Death in Sandpiper Bay

A Riley Harper Mystery, Volume 1

Traci Hall and Patrice Wilton

Published by Dreamscape Press, 2021.

DEATH IN SANDPIPER BAY

First edition. June 22, 2021.

Copyright © 2021 Traci Hall and Patrice Wilton.

ISBN: 979-8201624828

Written by Traci Hall and Patrice Wilton.

DEATH IN SANDPIPER BAY
A RILEY HARPER MYSTERY
by
TRACI HALL and PATRICE WILTON

There was a legend attached to idyllic Sandpiper Bay; a secret whispered from generation to generation. Summer folks were intrigued by the murmurs of haunts. Teenagers armed with flashlights searched the woods for spooky ghosts. Locals knew the rumors to have a grain of truth and stayed away from the forest. *Don't mess with it...it won't mess with you.*

Sixteen months ago, Police Officer Riley Harper and her partner were on surveillance in downtown Phoenix. The suspect rushed from his apartment building, hands raised, when her partner fired and shot the man in the chest. It was a bad kill and she'd had to testify against her former brother-in-arms. Labeled a snitch, Riley has been bombarded by the police, the media, and her former friends. Her reputation is in tatters and her career in Phoenix over. On leave since then, she's only had one job offer...from a place called Sandpiper Bay, a remote island off the coast of Maine. Riley expects an uncomplicated life for her mother, and her daughter, who moved with her. Nothing more dangerous than settling feuds among the fishermen. She is dead wrong.

DEDICATION
We'd like to thank Annie Beck, who talked about a remote island off the coast of Maine with a full-time population of around a thousand residents, and triple that in summer months. The only means to the island was a ferry service or private boat. This sparked the idea for a mystery series and Death in Sandpiper Bay was born.

A special thank you to all the fans out there who have read and enjoyed our Salem B&B cozy mystery series published with Kensington, and our "Charlene" fan club. We hope you'll follow us over to Maine.

Thank you!
Patrice Wilton and Traci Hall

PRAISE FOR OUR "SALEM B&B COZY MYSTERY SERIES"
Mrs. Morris and the Ghost

"Once I started reading, I couldn't put it down! I'm psyched that I discovered this book just in time for the next one. Highly entertaining, incredibly fun read!"

"This mystery has everything.. fun, love, heartache and suspense! I enjoyed reading and trying to help solve the mystery right along with Mrs. Morris! Can't wait to read another ghost story in this series!"

"I loved this book from the very first page. It was entertaining, the characters were enjoyable, there were surprises along the way and it is written so well."

"Compelling characters to a well plotted mystery create an engaging read."

Mrs. Morris and the Witch

"The mystery was well- crafted, with plenty of suspense and red herrings to keep me guessing. I highly recommend this one."

I loved this book. I mean, absolutely loved this book. The Salem B & B Mystery series is fast tracking it's way to my favorite cozy series of all time. It was a fabulous read and I can't wait to see what happens next!

How absolutely entertaining! Charlene Morris owns a B&B in Salem and has her own resident ghost. These books are exceptionally well written with fabulous characters. Upon reading these books I feel like I am in Salem visiting all the sights described within. I hope there are many, many more books to come in this series. Highly recommended!!

Mrs. Morris and the Ghost of Christmas Past

"This is one of the most entertaining series I've read! Extremely well written with great characterization. If you want to leave "real life" behind pick up this book and laugh or gasp or cry or just enjoy the read. Enjoy!"

"This series is just plain awesome!! I love the characters! I love the setting! The B&B is a place I would love to visit and stay at. Just love it all!"

"The Salem B&B Mysteries is quickly becoming one of my favorite cozy mystery series. I enjoyed this third book immensely. The characters are engaging, the setting charming, and I was unable to solve the mystery, which is always a plus. The writing style flows effortlessly and the wintry Christmas atmosphere will leave you longing for the holiday season."

Chapter One

Riley Harper clung to the slick railing of the Sandpiper Bay ferry as swirling white caps pounded repeatedly against the steel hull. This was no sleek vessel to cross smooth waters, but an iron and steel barge meant to withstand harsh conditions. These days she identified with the barge.

She glanced back at her mom, Susan, who huddled on a steel bench with Kyra, Riley's fourteen-year-old daughter. Kyra's skin had a green tinge as she crossed her arms over her belly. Susan patted Kyra's back. The past two days of travel from Phoenix had been a series of misadventures compounded by Kyra's pouting resistance. Riley understood. Kyra had been forced to leave behind her friends, her school, her home, all so that Riley could take a job as a police officer on a remote island.

Poor darling snuggled next to her grandma, her tears mingling with the unrelenting wind as the ferry plowed ahead. Riley signaled for them to join her for some fresh air. With seeming reluctance, the two gave up their middle row bench and weaved their way past other people to the rail.

"Are you okay, hon?" She touched her daughter's forehead, noting that it was damp with sweat, her flesh clammy. "Keep your eyes on the horizon. It will help you get your equilibrium back and you'll feel better."

"Take deep breaths. See that patch of blue beyond the rocks? We'll be out of this soon," her mom said to Kyra. As a career neo-natal nurse, Susan Meyers had a calming influence on most anyone, especially her beloved granddaughter.

Kyra lifted her face to the brisk gusts, her long brown braid fluttering back. "I don't feel good."

"I'm sorry, sweet pea." Riley gave her daughter a brief hug and kiss on her head before she could pull away. "This journey has not had an auspicious start. But what do you do when life gives you lemons?"

Kyra rolled her eyes. "Make lemonade. So lame. I don't see it getting better if the last two days are anything to go by."

Riley winced and tried not to dwell on the awful flight, lost luggage, or spooky hotel. "We're moving forward." The front of the ferry hit a rough chop. The barge lifted about four feet and then dropped, covering them all with sea spray.

"Seriously?" Her daughter's voice exuded affronted teenager. "You book us a room in a place that's scarier than the *Bates Motel*. I wasn't the only one to skip a shower this morning." Kyra raised a fist and grimaced like a madwoman as she made stabbing motions in the air. "Ca-reepy!"

"It *was* a tiny bathroom reminiscent of *Psycho*. It even had the white shower curtain." Riley rubbed the chill from her arms.

"Maybe we should all think of this as an adventure," Susan suggested. Riley's mom always gave everything a positive spin.

"Forget lemonade. This move is a mistake." Kyra repeated the stabbing motion, then closed her eyes and stuck out her tongue as if she'd fainted.

Susan laughed at Kyra's dramatics.

Riley hoped her daughter was wrong about that but to be fair, things hadn't been smooth.

A traffic jam near the Phoenix airport had caused them to be late for their flight, but they'd run and made the gate just as it was closing. Kyra had lost her headphones in the race to the plane and had been miserable without her music. When they landed, Riley bought Kyra a new pair to keep her happy, conscious of the bank account but deciding the purchase was worth it.

With a three-hour wait in Dallas for their plane to Boston, the trio shared a cheese pizza with a soggy crust before boarding. They were too hungry to complain. Good thing they'd eaten, as they were only offered an expensive snack menu during their four-hour flight. The grand finale was a commuter plane to Knox County with twenty-four passenger seats, small overhead bins, and pencil-thin aisles.

They were shaken but not stirred for the half-hour bumpy flight, where they were to catch a ferry in the morning to Sandpiper Bay. Somewhere along the way, they'd lost Riley's suitcase, but the airline promised to deliver it by morning to the hotel. Her mom had her bag, at least. Kyra had shared with Riley.

The "Bates", their nickname for the atrocity that awaited them, was built out of stone with one square window per room. Dark in color and in mood, it resembled something from a horror movie. Too frightened and wound up to sleep, they'd played cards, told scary stories, and giggled until daylight. Riley's suitcase, scratched and dented, was in the lobby when they checked out.

"Fine," Riley conceded. "Maybe lemonade is too much to ask for. I just hope that the bad times are behind us."

Her mom and her daughter both nodded vigorously. Kyra gulped and kept her eyes on the horizon, snugged between Riley and Susan for warmth. They'd all dressed for summer in shorts and thin T-shirts—which didn't cut it here on the ferry.

Fifteen minutes later, Captain Wyatt steered the barge away from the protrusion of rocks that formulated uninhabited islands, toward a protected waterway. It was like stepping into a new world; the waves flattened as smooth as Lake Pleasant and sunlight flickered through the swift-moving clouds.

The captain's deep tones bellowed over the speakers. "It's a lot less bumpy from here on out, folks."

"It better be," Kyra muttered, one hand on the railing, the other on her tummy.

Relishing the reprieve, Riley snapped pictures of the area with her cell phone. Shamrock-green patches of land covered the bigger islands. Dozens of lighthouses dotted the rugged coast.

"There are so many lighthouses!" Susan said.

Riley had read up on the remarkable structures after seeing the white and red Sandpiper Bay Lighthouse on the island's website. "Aren't they great? Some of them are over a hundred years old and still in service, guiding cargo ships and sailors through fog and hurricane-strength storms to a safe harbor."

Kyra shrugged and turned her back on the water to scan the crowds around them. Unimpressed...or pretending to be.

Susan nudged her but got no response. "Come on, Kyra. You have to admit the scenery is beautiful. Nothing like this in Phoenix. Can you imagine a lighthouse in the desert? Think about the stories you'll tell your friends when you get back home!"

She flinched at her mother's innocent remark. Riley had sold her three-bedroom home in Phoenix when she'd gotten the job here. The contract was for a year. Who knew where they would end up after she proved herself a worthy cop, but it was doubtful she would ever call Phoenix home again. Too much bad blood.

"Mom made sure we can't go back." With her nose in the air, Kyra turned and moved a few feet away from Riley. Riley felt miscast as the Disney villain when she wanted to be the hero.

Kyra's anger was magnified by her shame of her mother, which caused a deep, helpless ache inside. Being labeled a snitch by the police force that had once held her in high regard had destroyed them. Kyra didn't understand why she wasn't invited to her friends' houses, or worse, maybe she did. Riley hated that she'd been forced to testify against a man she'd considered a brother-in-arms. Family. Her conscience, and Kyra's safety, demanded she follow through and do the right thing.

Kyra stepped closer to Susan, who smoothed back a wisp of Kyra's long brown hair. Forehead to forehead, the two had an animated but whispered conversation. Their words were caught in the wind and her stomach tightened.

"...I could sue for emancipation. I'm fourteen!"

"Kyra. How would you support yourself?"

"I can get a job at the Phoenix bowling alley. I'd be free to do whatever I want and not be forced to spend a year in exile."

Riley's breath caught as her mother stayed calm and smiled softly at Kyra. "Do you have any idea how that would affect not only your life and well-being, but that of your mother's and mine?"

"I already hate it here." Kyra's lower lip jutted. "Can I really do that?"

"You come from a long line of strong women who don't quit. They don't give up on their families because things are hard. Your mother and I love you so much that if you *chose* to leave us, it would break our hearts."

Riley's heart thundered and her nose stung. Her daughter wanted to be free of her? Had she made the wrong decision? It wasn't as if there'd been job offers lined up after she'd testified. She'd had to take this job or give up being a cop, which was all she'd ever wanted to be.

Kyra kept her head bowed and whispered something Riley couldn't catch.

Susan leaned her elbow on the rail behind her. "If you let it, this can be quite the adventure. Someday, when you're much older, as old as me, you'll look back at this year with fond memories."

"I doubt that. No friends, new school. Might as well kill me now."

"Don't say that," her mother said fiercely. "Give this place a chance, give your mom a chance. She isn't trying to ruin your life...she's providing for you. It hasn't been easy for her either."

Riley sent her mom a grateful smile from four feet away.

Kyra, back to Riley, gave a small nod. "Okay. But if I still hate it later, maybe I could live with Sammy?" Kyra's best friend in Phoenix had taken the news of the move hard, and the girls had been inseparable for the past month.

Susan veered the subject away from Sammy. "I can't wait to see the cottage. Four bedrooms? We will each have plenty of space. I'm ready to try new things."

"Like what?" Kyra's petulant voice made it clear that she wasn't letting go of her reservations.

"Well, we've never lived next to a bay before. I'd love to rent a boat and water-ski. And learn to kayak. That seems like fun. I know you'd be great."

Kyra laughed. "No way, Nana! You, water-skiing? I can't even imagine it."

"I did as a young girl. My parents took my sister and me camping every summer for a few weeks. We rented a boat and had the best time."

Riley's heart lightened as Kyra smiled and tossed her side braid over her shoulder. Her dark-brown hair was highlighted from the Arizona sun. "I don't know, Nana. I prefer a nice, chlorinated pool. There's snakes and gators and all kinds of creatures lurking beneath the surface. I saw *Lake Placid* three times."

"Nonsense!" Susan snorted. "You might be too young to remember, but when you were five, Gramps and I took you to Maui for a vacation. You loved the ocean. You were fearless and as slippery as a dolphin when we tried to catch you to go back to the hotel." She laughed and tickled her granddaughter on her exposed tummy, avoiding the silver naval ring she'd had done with Sammy before leaving.

"Stop that, Nana." Kyra's mouth twitched as she tried to keep a straight face. "You know how much I hate to be tickled."

"Admit this is going to be fun. We'll be able to try new things. Think of it as an extended holiday."

Kyra giggled and squirmed. "Nana!"

Susan stopped tormenting Kyra and put her hands in the air, her smile fading. "All right. I'll stop...but I want you to know that we love you very much. When you get overwhelmed or sad or lonely, you can always talk to me, okay?"

Her mother glanced her way, and Riley nodded her appreciation. Her mother had moved with them, no hesitation at all when Riley had asked for her help. Unlike Riley, Susan had rented out her condo rather than sell.

One year.

Would the Phoenix police department forget her sins in that amount of time? Accusations of disloyalty from her fellow officers had made staying there impossible. TV, the papers, the trial, and the verdict had all portrayed her as a cop condemning another cop, though she'd done the right thing. She'd been thrown to the wolves by the same people who should've had her back.

She'd hoped to make a new start in Sandpiper Bay where people wouldn't whisper or give her snide glances. Where she'd be judged on her own performance and behavior. Yet she'd heard the doubt in the chief's voice when he'd confirmed the position was hers, and she knew in her bones that she'd have to fight for his respect.

"How much longer, Mom?" Kyra appeared at her side, lifting her hand to shade her eyes. Her skin had lost the goosebumps at last beneath the August sun and the subdued breeze off the water. The light-blue midi T-shirt showed off a young woman's figure. Her shorts revealed long legs. Riley hoped that she had a chance to preserve Kyra's innocence here on the island, away from the fast pace of the city.

She checked the ferry schedule and the time on her phone. "Another twenty minutes, sweetheart." Riley wouldn't let her daughter know that her feelings had been hurt by her careless words. "Are you getting anxious for our first view?"

"Hardly. I'm just hoping the stuff we shipped here has arrived already. I need my winter clothes even though it's summer."

"It should be there now." Riley gave her a hug and prayed that their things weren't lost like her luggage had been. "While you and Nana were chatting like squirrels, you missed several small islands that I think we can explore. There will be so much to do here! Oh, look at that seagull dive for lunch!"

The bird flew straight down into the murky water and pulled out a wriggling fish. It gulped half down.

"Gross!" Kyra squinted. "Its fins are still flapping."

"It's the way of the world, I'm afraid. The strong survive, and the weak get eaten." Riley gave a chomp.

Kyra laughed in surprise. "What happened to being positive? Lemonade out of lemons?"

She raised her hands and grinned at her daughter. "We are strong, you and me, and won't get eaten. That's a fact."

Kyla scrunched her nose in doubt. "I'm kinda skinny, and you aren't much bigger, Mom."

It was true that at five-four, Riley was only a hundred and twenty pounds, thanks to the Stress Diet, but she was tough...so was Kyra, to handle the last year without letting her grades slip. She saved her moods for her mother. "We have determination and willpower, and that makes us formidable opponents in the game of life."

Kyra snickered. "Have you been drinking?"

"Kyra!" Riley hooked her arm through her daughter's, happy they weren't arguing. "Please don't make up your mind about Sandpiper Bay until you've been there awhile. I have a good feeling about it." She let her gaze go to the surrounding sea. "I've never seen water like this before, emerald in some places, dark blue in others."

"We could have seen it on Instagram instead of moving here." Tossing her long thick braid over one shoulder, Kyra took a step back.

So much for the warm fuzzies.

Riley reached for her hand, hoping she wouldn't shake it off. "I'm sorry that you're unhappy, but I promise the time will go fast. Next month you'll be going to school with the other kids off the island. Taking a ferry every day—how cool is that?"

"I prefer a school bus."

"Boring! Maybe Nana can go with you at first? Until you get settled. You'll be able to get all your homework done before you reach home." She tried to be upbeat for her daughter's sake, but it was hard work.

"I don't need a babysitter. I can take care of myself." Kyra put one hand on her hip. "I don't want Nana to come with me. Forget it."

Riley gritted her teeth. "We'll find out more now that we're here." The town website had been confusing with a lot of options regarding schooling. "There's a small school on the island and a big one on the mainland. I just thought you'd like the mainland so you could be at a high school with kids your own age."

"Kids I don't know. And don't want to know." Kyra nibbled her lower lip, the nervous gesture belying the hard words.

"You'll make friends right off the bat. They'll want to know all about Phoenix and you."

"Why would they want that?"

"Kyra! You're funny and smart. So pretty. I'm sure you'll have them totally entertained with stories about the red mountains and the rattlers. Coyotes. I bet they've never seen a cactus. Or a dust devil."

"I can't believe you took me away from all that."

"We didn't have much choice, sweetheart."

"You didn't! But I could have stayed."

"You're only fourteen. You still need Nana and me."

"You're not the one leaving friends behind."

That comment stung, and she slipped on her sunglasses to hide her hurt. It was true. She had no friends in Phoenix anymore, or on the police force, and her inner circle had turned their backs as well.

Susan joined them, her hand on Riley's shoulder as she peered over the side. "That water is sure pretty, isn't it?"

"It is, Mom." Riley patted her mom's fingers. Captain Wyatt announced the name of an island they passed but she didn't catch it. Green trees, rugged terrain that sloped down to small private beaches, the coves alive with fishing boats, kayakers, and friendly people who waved at the passengers on the ferry. Would this ever feel like home? Or was she just like her daughter and simply biding her time?

Kyra moved a few feet away, her nose down as she texted on her cell phone. Probably complaining to Sammy.

"My own daughter hates me."

Susan smiled at Riley. "You know that's not true. She's testy right now, but she's giving up a lot, not starting high school with her friends. Be patient. Let her have her moody moments and give her space to sort it all out."

"I am. *I will*. I'm trying."

The engine of the barge slowed as they neared Sandpiper Bay.

"To the left," Captain Wyatt boomed, "you'll see the seals common to the island. Seals can be quite large. Some say sailors mistook them for mermaids. Ugly woman, cute seal."

Riley reached for Kyra and grinned at the frolicking seals. At least twenty glided around the ferry, dipping in and out of the water. "They're showing off!"

Other passengers had left the cabin below and were hugging the rails. Susan and Kyra had to squeeze into the space Riley had been saving. Kyra laughed and snapped photos of the seals. "They're adorable! Sammy won't believe it!"

Her joy brought tears to Riley's eyes. Just maybe things would be all right.

A bystander in cargo shorts and a T-shirt that advertised The Shack said, "Those are harbor seals." His laid-back attitude made him approachable. Was he a knowledgeable tourist or a local? "We've got two kinds around here. The gray seal is much larger, thick in body, and not very sociable. Darker in color too. These guys are friendly."

His light-brown hair was shaggy, and he had scruff on his square jaw. Cobalt eyes reflected the sea around them. He'd said "we" which meant he probably lived here.

Kyra gave him a big smile. "What else can you tell us about this place?"

"Well"—he ruffled his hair—"you doin' a day trip on Sandpiper Bay or spending a few nights?"

Just then Riley spied the island that would be their temporary home. "Look!" She pointed to a patch of land with colorful cottages painted in bright hues, a forest of trees, and numerous fishing boats bobbing in the coves around it.

"Do you see it, Kyra?" Riley grinned at her daughter.

"Yeah, Mom." Kyra's chin hefted. "The whole place is smaller than our old neighborhood. And it stinks like fish."

"The scent of fish grows on you after a while," the man said with a chuckle. "I've lived on the island for four years now and don't even notice." He pointed to his shirt. "I own the bar. Best fish and chips around."

Riley's stomach growled. It was close to one in the afternoon, and she was ready for lunch.

The water turned choppy and seagulls flew overhead. Susan brought out a pair of binoculars from her handbag and focused them on the dock. Her bright smile faded quickly. "It does look awfully tiny, doesn't it?"

Kyra nodded and sucked in her lower lip. "How can we live here for a year, Mom?"

"A year?" The man wore a confused expression.

Riley offered her hand. "I'm Riley Harper, this is my daughter Kyra and my mom, Susan."

"Coby Jenkins. People go by first names around here." He looked at Riley for a moment too long.

Riley decided to set him straight—she had no interest in flirtations. "I'm joining your police force starting tomorrow. I'll be *Officer* Harper."

He laughed and scratched the bristles on his jaw. "Seriously? If that's the case, you can arrest me anytime."

She kept a polite smile on her face. "I don't take my job as an officer of the law lightheartedly."

Her daughter glanced curiously from Coby to Riley.

"Sorry," Coby said in his too-charming way. "Bad joke. You met the chief yet?"

"Just over the internet during our online interview." Chief Barnes had been stiff and formal. "He said he would pick us up at the ferry dock. I asked about a rental car, but the island doesn't have a service?"

"There are business cards for taxis in the ferry depot. Also brochures for restaurants and that kind of thing. See that guy over there?" He pointed and the three women turned.

A blond man with a silver hoop in his brow Coby waved and smiled at them when he saw them looking. He wore a polo shirt that read Sandpiper Bay Ferry.

"That's Deke Anderson. He works six days a week for Captain Wyatt and knows just about everybody. He's a local boy. He can help you, if the chief isn't...as...amenable."

Alarms went off in Riley's head. The chief wasn't a friendly man and everybody knew it. At least not friendly toward Riley. She hadn't even disembarked and was already in trouble.

"Oh, great!" Kyra groaned. "A crabby chief, a pint-size island. Yay, us."

Coby's deep-blue eyes crinkled at the corners. "You just wait, Kyra. This place has a way of growing on you. One year in paradise and you'll never want to leave."

Chapter Two

Riley lurched forward as the ferry banged into the wooden dock. Deke tied up to a tall post, and Captain Wyatt thanked everyone over the speakers. "If you checked luggage, it will be brought to the green canopy in front of the depot."

"Do they sell frequent flyer passes?" Kyra asked Coby with a half-smile.

"They do, inside." Coby pointed to a single-story wood and glass building to the right of the dock. "By the month, or by the year. That's cheapest."

Captain Wyatt left the glass-enclosed area where he steered the ferry and walked through the throng on deck waiting to get off. He opened the metal gate and ushered everyone down a metal plank wide enough for two people across.

Coby went down first, then Riley, then Kyra and Susan. In the grass area, Coby stuck his hands in his faded jean pockets and glanced around the milling folks. "Don't see the chief yet. Maybe he's cracking a big case. Lots of crime around here."

Riley gave him a steely look. "Another bad joke?"

"Yeah." Coby rubbed his shaggy hair. "I have plenty."

"I bet you do." She stepped aside to where the bags were being dragged off a large cart by a burly, oversized man who tossed them on the ground as if they were sacks of oats.

"These yours?" the burly man spat to the right, into the grass. Kyra's eyes widened in shock.

"Yes." Riley quickly grabbed the two suitcases and set them upright, swiping at the dirt. The generous tip she'd planned to give the man would stay snug in her pocket.

Coby whistled and took hold of the larger suitcase, wheeling it away from the ferry to a bench across from the street with chipped paint and a fluttering seagull perched at one end. "Might as well sit here and wait for Barnes to show up. I'd wait with you, but I've got to get to the bar. I had a late start today. Dentist appointment." He hooked his thumb down the dusty street. "It's the rust-colored building with the blue sign out front, says 'The Shack.' There's only one in town."

"Another bad joke?" Riley arched her eyebrow.

"No. The truth, ma'am, nothing but the truth. My bar is the only shack around—best fish and chips, largest selection of beer on tap."

She had to smile at his relentless good cheer. "I'm sure we'll be visiting soon."

"Better yet, you can come along with me now. How does a cool drink sound until your ride shows up? Time can be a little fluid on the island."

"Please, Mom?" Kyra folded her hands in a silent plea and put her best smile on. Was this act for the cute man standing in front of them? He had to be double her age, so Kyra better not get that into her fuzzy head.

"I think we'd better wait here for the chief." She didn't want to make a worse impression by not being where they'd arranged for her to be.

Susan bobbed her head toward a run-down house across the street where a man of indeterminate age sat in a fold-up chair stroking a chicken. "That's an interesting sight," she murmured. "Is that Sandpiper Bay's version of old folks in Florida sitting on their porch and waiting to die?"

"Mom!"

Coby snickered.

Riley fanned her face with her floppy hat, then put it back on her head. That was not a positive observation and very unlike her mother. "Once we get to our cabin, everything will be brighter."

"Yeah?" Kyra perched on the edge of the bench and picked at her blue fingernail. "Is all this going to disappear?" She looked at Coby with disappointment. "How can you stand it here?"

He shrugged uncomfortably. "It grows on you."

"Yeah? So does lice."

"Kyra!" Riley glared at her daughter, then her mother. "Where are your manners?"

Susan, red-faced, smiled at Coby. "Sorry. We're all a little cranky after what we've been through to get here. We will be in a better place after a good night's sleep. I'll take a raincheck on the cool drink."

Coby backed away, hands in the air. "You've got it. Ladies, let me be the first to officially welcome you to our special island. Trust me, Kyra, you'll see it for yourself one day."

A tear rolled down Kyra's cheek, proof of how exhausted her daughter was. "You promise?"

"I do." Coby hiked his shoulders and whistled the tune of "Don't Worry, Be Happy" by Bobby McFerrin, giving Riley a wink.

She remained stone-faced. The last thing she needed was to encourage this handsome charmer and be the talk of the town. "Okay, everyone. I have the address for the cottage. Should we stay here, or start pulling our bags down the street?"

"Stay put," Susan declared, folding her arms and looking a little disgruntled. They all were. No one had slept last night, and their expectations had dimmed after their first initial sighting of an island they were condemned to for an entire year.

Was this to be her prison sentence for a crime not committed?

"I suggest we wait as well." Riley checked the time on her cell phone. Where was Bradley Barnes anyway? The ferry had arrived fifteen minutes ago!

"How far is it?" Kyra's shoulders slumped as she gave a weary glance at the few islanders who passed by. Chicken-man remained on his front porch. The locals on bikes or walking wished the ladies a good afternoon like a neighborhood greeting committee.

"At least the people are welcoming and pleasant, which is more than I can say about the present company, myself included." Susan shook her head. "I think we all need a shower and a good rest, then we'll have a better outlook on things."

"You're right, Mom." Riley straightened and forced a bright smile. "I did my research before I agreed to this position and it has a lot to offer. Matter-of-fact, Sandpiper Bay is a favorite summer spot for the mainlanders." She shrugged. "They *choose* to come here, year after year."

Kyra stuck a stick of gum in her mouth and made smacking noises.

Ignoring her, Riley continued. "We might be remote, but there is a decent market that carries everything the residents need. They'll even order special items on request, which will be delivered the very next day."

"Oh great!" Kyra chewed and smacked. "Will they deliver pizza or Chinese?"

"Who knows? Maybe." The ferry ride had taken thirty minutes. They could always go to the mainland for an outing. She tapped her toe on the ground, getting a little concerned. Was the chief going to show up or not? Should they get a business card from the ferry depot for a taxi? Should they walk? Her bones ached she was so tired from lack of sleep.

"That's nice to know, Riley." Susan gripped the handle of her suitcase. "I sure love my ice cream."

Riley bowed her head to hide a chuckle. Her mom was thin but had a sweet tooth. "This entire island is only twelve miles long and eight miles wide but still, it's got plenty of restaurants. Two with great reviews. One Italian and the other is a seafood place on a wharf overlooking the water. They have a medical center, a one-person post office, some touristy shops, and a bank with an ATM."

"Whoopie!" Kyra said sarcastically.

"Okay, okay, it's not what we're accustomed to, but the place is very beautiful. We can start exploring after lunch and a few hours' sleep." She removed her hat as she was getting warm. "It's quaint, but everyone has been friendly, and I think we need to give it a chance."

"Of course," Susan agreed. "I'm excited to be here."

Riley gave her mom a warm smile. "There's more. It has its own lighthouse. A marina with fresh fish every day. Clear coves for swimming or fishing, and a volunteer fire department. Not to forget a three-officer police force."

"What about the chief?" Susan asked. "Will he be retiring soon?"

"Not that I know of." Riley blew out a hot breath. Should she go into the depot and buy some water?

"I bet you're at least equal to him in experience and training. You've got fifteen years in. What if you like it and want to stay?"

"I'd like to hear the answer to that," a deep voice rumbled. "Sorry I'm late—had

to pick up a few things."

Mortified by the conversation he'd overheard, Riley turned on her heel and met her boss for the first time, if you didn't count the one and only Zoom meeting that had sealed the deal.

Graying hair had been brushed back from his forehead and revealed deep grooves as if the man worried a lot. He was thick around the middle, his stomach protruding the single button of his brown suit jacket. Dark-brown slacks, brown leather shoes.

"Chief Bradley Barnes, it's nice to meet you in person." His hands were large and when he shook Riley's in greeting, hers was lost. He squeezed once and released. Her skin stung but she didn't complain. "My daughter, Kyra, and my mother, Susan. I won't be answering that last question!" She laughed to try and make a joke of it, but he only frowned.

Sour grapes.

His scowl deepened. "Let me take your suitcase, if you can manage the smaller one?" He didn't wait for them to answer but snagged the handle of her bag from her loose grip and started across the street where a blue SUV was parked.

Hmm. She glanced back at her mom, who's mouth had dropped open, and her daughter, who had sucked in a breath. Since her boss had her suitcase, she reached for her mother's. "Come on, ladies. Or we might miss our ride."

That got them moving.

Barnes opened the back hatch of the SUV and placed her suitcase in with barely more care than the man from the ferry. "I expect you'll settle in real soon."

She read the subtext. He wouldn't be coddling them. Barnes swung in the last suitcase and slammed it shut. "Get on in," he said.

Riley opened the passenger door and climbed up, as her mom and Kyra settled themselves in the back. Barnes started the engine and pressed on the gas. The car was in park, or they might have ended up on the porch with the chicken man, who grinned and kept patting the docile fowl.

"What do you think?" Barnes checked his mirrors and pulled onto the street. There was little traffic.

"About what?" Riley hoped he didn't want her first impression of the place or him. That wouldn't win her any brownie points. The string of bad luck appeared to be going strong.

"The trip over. Sandpiper Bay—not that you've seen anything much except the harbor. Though I don't suppose they have oceans in Phoenix?" His mouth twitched. Was he having fun at her expense?

Kyra sat forward from her position behind the chief. "Why does that old man sit and pet his chicken near the ferry dock?"

Barnes shrugged. "Same answer as to why the chicken crosses the road."

Kyra jerked back, arms crossed. Susan poked her head between the seats. "What? To get to the other side? That doesn't make sense."

"No." Barnes actually grinned at Susan. "Because he can."

Susan laughed, then stopped abruptly when she noticed that no one else thought it was funny. An awkward silence grew.

Riley cleared her throat and started a mental list of things to discuss with her family once they were all settled. "How long have you lived here, Chief Barnes?" She kept her tone respectful.

"Three years. The missus and I moved here after our girls were in college."

"From?" Susan asked.

"Portland."

Kyra's voice lifted at someplace she recognized. "Oregon?"

"Maine." Barnes turned right. "Shelley, my wife, wants to go back. We just became grandparents a short while ago." He allowed a real smile at that but kept his gaze on the road.

So maybe he did want to retire and that could be the reason he'd hired her—she was nowhere near ready to hang up her badge. However, her contract was only for a year. Riley shot her mother a glance. *Don't say a word.*

"Congratulations," Riley said. "Boy or girl?"

"Twin girls," he answered proudly.

"I'll double that congratulations!" Susan briefly touched his shoulder from her seat in the back. "I worked with babies most of my life. I was an administrator and head nurse in the neonatal department. I put in thirty years and loved it very much."

"The girls were five pounds each and healthy as can be. They're growing so fast!"

"You are truly blessed." Susan smiled and turned her head to stare out the window at the passing cottages by the harbor. "These are so sweet."

Kyra plugged in her earbuds to tune out any conversation.

Within five minutes, they'd turned off the main street to a smaller paved road.

"Here we are," Barnes said, slowing as he passed the front to drive around the back.

The multi-level robin's egg blue cabin wasn't rustic in any way. The darker blue of the open bay behind it peeked through evergreen trees. Riley's heart sang with excitement. It was beyond her expectations, better than the photos. And the way her luck had been, she'd had low expectations. "It's gorgeous," she exclaimed. "What do you say, Mom, Kyra?"

"It's so big!" her mother exclaimed, her hand to her chest. "There will be plenty of room for us all."

"It's okay, I guess." Kyra tugged out one earbud and wrapped a piece of her hair loose from her braid around a finger. "The deck looks cool."

Bradley raised a brow and glanced at Riley in response to Kyra's attitude. He should know all about teen girls. "This is one of the finest rentals on Sandpiper Bay." He parked at the rear entrance that had a garage snugged up next to the house. "You were lucky to get this. Most places close up for the winter, but your offer arrived just in time."

She could use a little luck. If the inside was as amazing as the outside, then she'd say the trip over had been worth it, lack of sleep and creepy hotel included.

They all jumped out of the SUV. Bradley opened the back hatch and pulled out the suitcases, taking the largest and handing Riley the other.

"I've got the key." He pulled a bright-blue dolphin keychain from his pocket and unlocked the door. "After you."

Susan smiled politely at Barnes and tugged Kyra behind her into the cabin. Riley's stomach clenched when her mother gasped.

"What?" She hurried through the back mudroom.

Susan spun around with her arms spread, a smile of wonder on her face. "It's amazing! Look at the vaulted ceiling with skylights. We can see the fir trees and sunlight flickering in. Maybe even the moon at night. Happy days are here again."

Riley laughed and left the suitcase by the door.

Kyra leaned against a large picture window, forehead to the glass. "There's a canoe down there, and a rowboat too. I wonder if we have neighbors?"

"Yep," Barnes answered. "On either side, but the lots are a quarter acre."

"Big enough for a garden," her mom said.

"And a hammock where we can read beneath the trees!" Kyra twirled toward Riley with sparkling eyes.

Riley sighed with pleasure. She had been afraid that this might disappoint them too.

She walked around in a daze, taking it all in. "The picture of the fireplace on the website didn't do it justice. It's huge! I can see us spending our evenings together, with hot chocolate and popcorn on these couches. What do you think?"

"Is there a TV?" Kyra asked with a hint of concern.

"It's in the cabinet." Riley opened a wooden door to reveal a large flatscreen. "I read that they have games and DVDs too."

"The furnishings are also very nice." Susan touched the fabric on one of the two matching sofas. "Well kept and quite new."

"Better than our old couch," Kyra agreed as she plopped down onto one of them.

The yellow-and-blue-striped sofas faced each other with a square carved wood table in the center. To the left was the stone fireplace. Another two plush chairs were set next to the front windows, allowing them to enjoy the view or spend an afternoon with a good book. A small rattan table nestled between them, and a standing lamp by the curtains angled to where the light was needed. This, Riley thought with relief, was an oasis at last.

Riley turned as Barnes stomped back into the house from the SUV, juggling two large paper bags that he dumped on the kitchen counter. She hoped whatever was inside wasn't fragile.

"I got you some supplies for the next day or two until you can do a more thorough shopping at the market," he said gruffly.

"That was so kind of you," Riley told him. Is that what had made him late? She could look past the tardiness since he'd been doing them a favor, but he was still damn hard to read.

He dipped his head. "Shelley suggested it. Had to drive past the market on the way to get you so I picked up some necessities, not much, but it'll save you from having to go today. Expect you're all mighty tired."

"I am!" Kyra poked into the closest bag. "Cookies! Yeah!" She smiled at him. "Thanks, Chief Barnes. Are we allowed to use the boat down by the water?"

"Yep. They go with the cabin rental, and you have two bikes in the garage as well."

"That is awfully nice," Riley replied. Things were looking up for sure. She'd send the owners a message by email to thank them.

Kyra put down the cookie she was biting into, eyes wide with concern. "This is all great, but do we have internet?"

Barnes fought a smile. "It's limited out here, but we have a couple of hot spots in town which you can rely on. The library is a great place to connect."

Riley nodded at him in thanks. "This was very considerate of you and Shelley." She looked him square in the face as an equal, not a new hire that he had obvious reservations about. "I hate to keep you any longer from your day."

He placed the dolphin keychain on the counter next to the bags. "There's a map of the island on the kitchenette table. It'll give you the lay of the land."

Riley was so tired that it felt as if her feet were encased in wet cement, her eyelids heavy. "Thank you."

He stepped toward the door, then turned to say, "See you promptly at seven thirty tomorrow morning, Ms. Harper. Don't be late." He nodded to them all, and then he was gone.

Kyra had already opened the cabinet which hid the TV. Grabbing the remote, she turned it on, and sure enough the screen opened to a cooking show. Her daughter sprawled out on the couch, feet up.

Her mom dug out the supplies Barnes had brought, sorting them as she opened both bags as to what needed to be put in the fridge. Riley joined her. "This was thoughtful, don't you think? I'm trying to get a read on him."

"It was a kind gesture."

Riley propped her elbow on the counter. "His wife made him do it."

Susan laughed. "He's a family man, which is good. And look at all of this food."

"It's a huge spread, and I'm starving."

"We all are—let me get lunch started and you can sort the bedrooms out."

Riley raised her voice so Kyra could hear and pointed to the staircase. "We've got two queens upstairs with a full bath, and two smaller bedrooms here on this level. One has a double, the other twins."

"I want to be downstairs!" Kyra shouted from the couch.

Susan laughed. "Guess we'll be up, then. I don't mind."

Scanning the area, Riley got a bad feeling in her stomach. "I don't see our boxes from Phoenix. I'll go see if they are upstairs."

Susan put her hand on Riley's wrist. "We have what we need in our suitcases, so don't worry."

"You're right. I don't think I've ever been so beat!"

Riley climbed the stairs but the boxes hadn't yet arrived so she brought out her cell phone to track the package. No service. "No internet!"

She returned to the kitchen with a headshake, not wanting Kyra to be upset.

"We've got enough food here to last us a week," her mom said, showing her the loot. Tea and coffee for the morning with sugar packets and cream and milk. Eggs, slabs of ham, a fresh loaf of bread, butter, a spicy mustard, and a jar of mayonnaise. A box of spaghetti, prepared meatballs in the freezer, grated cheese, and a six pack of water. He'd even remembered her daughter with popcorn and cookies and a giant package of Doritos.

"Who wants a ham sandwich?" Riley asked over the noise of the TV. "Kyra, you good with that?"

"With what?" She didn't bother to turn her head.

"Sandpiper Bay's best-ever ham sandwich!" She and her mom exchanged smiles.

The volume on the TV lowered. "Thought we were having lobster," Kyra muttered.

The idea of leaving this cozy cabin made her want to weep. "Let's all get some sleep first and then decide what we want to do for dinner. Lunch first!" How did it get to be two already?

Her mother had started making hefty sandwiches, adding a handful of Doritos on the side. "Come and get it," she called out.

Kyra turned off the TV with a grumble.

Riley opened the fridge to put the supplies away, and there on the side of the door was a bottle of red and one of white. A six-pack of beer was pushed to the rear of the top shelf, along with a large soda bottle. "Mom, look at this."

"Beer for me, darling."

"I think I'll have one myself. Kyra?"

"Water, please."

They took their lunch outdoors and ate on the long covered patio. It was a lovely day in the mid-seventies with a blue sky and clouds that floated by. Giant fir trees sheltered the cabin, offering privacy plus shade. She'd never lived anywhere with such a great view.

Lazily, they munched on their food, enjoyed their drinks, and talked and laughed more than they had in a while.

When they returned indoors the happy mood continued. At least for a few minutes. Kyra started flipping through some old DVDs. "They're all *old* movies." She tossed them aside. "I've already seen a few several times."

Riley understood her daughter's mood—they were all very tired.

Susan idly picked one up and laughed. "Ever seen this?" It was *Blue Lagoon* starring Brooke Shields and Christopher Atkins.

"No. It looks hideous. What are they *wearing*?"

Susan waved the DVD. "I'll bet you a bag of popcorn that you'll love it."

While Susan figured out how the DVD player worked, Riley put a hand on Kyra's shoulder. "It's a cute movie. A story about first love."

"Yeah, okay." Kyra unbraided her knotted hair. "I'm game. What's the premise? Short version."

Susan sighed. "A pretty girl around your age and a young lad who were shipwrecked on an island, all alone for years."

"Was he cute?" Kyra asked.

Riley nodded, thinking back to the popular movie and the blond god. "Yes, matter-of-fact, he was."

"Then it wouldn't be so bad. Alone on an island with a hottie."

Riley sat on the couch next to Kyra. "They had to build a shelter and learn to fish. Fish for breakfast, lunch, and dinner."

"That wouldn't be great."

"And then you'd have to rub twigs together to make a fire and boil the ocean water to drink it. No iPhones, no iPads, no FaceTime, no restaurants or grocery stores, or anyone else to talk to. Yikes!"

"Do they fall in love?" Kyra asked.

"I believe they did." Susan shook her head. "The pickings were slim, unless they found a cute turtle." They laughed and Riley got off her comfortable sofa to make a bag of popcorn, the first in their new home. Knowing they would have many firsts gave her a warm feeling inside.

Chapter Three

A low hum of anxiety woke Riley before dawn. She lay in her comfy bed and allowed herself to acclimatize. They were finally here in Sandpiper Bay. This was her first day of work. The next year was about salvaging her career.

What could possibly go wrong?

She tossed the downy comforter back and opened the dove-gray curtain that covered her bedroom window. Yep. That water view was still there. Deep blue and gorgeous, even in the predawn light.

The trunks had arrived last evening at six and so they'd voted to stay in and unpack, eating the spaghetti and meatballs for dinner before collapsing early to sleep.

Riley brought out her yoga mat and stretched muscles tight from stress—releasing, breathing. Her biggest struggle? Accepting. She was working on it.

Thirty minutes later, she'd showered and dressed in her navy and tan Sandpiper Bay police uniform. Her hair was in a tight bun and her makeup minimal. She was here to do a job she was more than qualified to do.

Following the scent of coffee downstairs, she smiled at her mother in the kitchen. Susan was wrapped in a cotton robe and slippers against the chill, hugging her steaming coffee to her chest.

"Morning, Mom. Little bit different than Phoenix, isn't it?"

"You can say that again." A window in the kitchen showed green trees. "It's pretty though, all this nature." Susan passed a mug across the counter. "How are you feeling?"

"Nervous."

"That's to be expected." Susan set her mug down and opened the refrigerator. "Can I make you some eggs?"

"Sure. Thanks." Riley sipped the dark roast—the blend as unfamiliar as her surroundings. She sat at the small kitchen table. "What service."

"I figured you might need an extra boost on your first day into the station." Her mom rummaged through the cupboards until she found a frying pan. "Score!"

"You used to get up early on my first day of school too, to make a special breakfast." Riley smiled. "We haven't lived together in a long time."

"Twenty years," Susan agreed with a peek over her shoulder. "Don't worry, Riley. We'll all learn how to get along."

Riley watched her mom scoot around the kitchen, cracking eggs into the pan and popping bread into a toaster. Though retired, her mother remained slender with an active lifestyle. She walked three miles a day and did yoga.

Eggs sizzled in butter and within moments a plate with two eggs, ham, and toast was set before her. Riley's stomach rumbled. "Are you joining me?"

"I am." Her mom sat opposite her, butter melting on her toast. "While you're at work, and if Kyra is amenable, we might take those bicycles and explore the island."

"That sounds fun. I stuck the map on the fridge with a magnet. Don't want you to be bored."

Her mom's gray brow lifted. "Only boring people get bored."

Riley took a sip of coffee and smiled. "I know. I remember." It had been her mom's go-to response whenever preteen Riley had complained.

"Besides, there will be so much to see and do." Her mom put a little of the egg on her toast. "I look forward to snowy days curled up by the fireplace with a book."

"Maybe you can start a local book club here like you had in Phoenix."

"We'll see. My plan is to have no plan for a while and just be in the moment here with you and Kyra."

"That sounds very wise."

Her mom dimpled. "Finally, you see the truth."

They laughed and Riley finished her breakfast. "I might need to borrow one of those bikes if the chief doesn't pick me up this morning. I was too tired yesterday and forgot to ask about the car."

A car for her use was supposed to be included in the contract, but when Riley had checked the garage, there had been no vehicle.

Riley shouldered her purse and grabbed her phone. "See ya! I'll go wait outside."

"Good luck, hon. You've got this."

Feeling nervous, Riley paced in front of the cabin. Minutes later a blue four-door sedan pulled up before her, but Chief Barnes wasn't behind the wheel.

She went to the passenger side and peered down to smile at a ginger-haired man in his late twenties. He gave her a half wave and reached across the interior to open the door.

She pulled it back and slid in.

"Hi," he said with a friendly grin. "I'm Matthew Sniders. Officer Sniders." Pink tinted his cheekbones. "Chief asked me to pick you up."

"Morning." She shifted to face him better. "Riley Harper. I wondered how I was going to get to the station. I was so exhausted yesterday I didn't ask many questions."

"Your place is on my way, so it wasn't a problem."

"How far is the department?" She wondered if she should walk or bike to work.

"Six miles." He glanced at her with another smile. "You'll need a car."

"I appreciate the lift this morning." Riley buckled her seat belt. "Part of the job description was personal use of a vehicle. Hope it's there waiting for me."

Matthew drove with his eyes straight ahead, both hands on the wheel. "Yep. Chief will get you all sorted, I'm sure. How was your first night?"

"Good. The cabin is a mansion compared to our old house. Feels like we're on vacation, being on the water like that."

"Where are you from again?"

"Phoenix." She was sure that he knew about her history on the police force though he didn't say anything. It was how he didn't say anything that clued her in. That meant the chief had been talking, as she'd feared.

Probably complaining about his new hire. *Great.* She smiled at Matthew. "How long have you worked for the police?"

"Right out of Sandpiper Bay high school. Ten years? Always wanted to be a cop."

"Never felt the urge to travel, see what's out there?"

His cheeks darkened from pink to rose. "Well. I *have* been off to visit the bigger cities, like Portland. Went to Boston for a weekend, saw all the sights, that kind of thing." He shrugged. "I prefer this. It's home."

The idea of being on this strip of water-locked land forever was unfathomable, but he seemed at ease with it. "I'm sure your family was happy you didn't take a job elsewhere."

"Yep. Mom and Dad still live in the same house my dad grew up in. I live in a cottage down the road and we have Sunday dinners together."

"Nice. Are you married?"

"I was engaged to my high school sweetheart, but Mindy decided to move to Boston. Hence the reason for my trip." He winked at Riley. "It didn't work out. It wasn't just for the job opportunities like she said. She wanted to find someone else. She knew I wanted to stay here. Retire here. Die here."

Riley flinched. "You're way too young to think of that. Besides, maybe five years from now you might decide to flutter your wings and see how the rest of the world lives."

He laughed but in a kind way that showed maturity. "Not everybody feels the same, but there are a thousand folks who live on this island year-round who probably agree with me. Sandpiper Bay is paradise."

As he said that they rounded a corner, and the ocean came into full view. Large boulders lined the rocky beach, and a white and red lighthouse in the distance beckoned to be explored.

"That is lovely. I don't know if I'll get used to seeing lighthouses and the ocean instead of red mountains and cactus."

Matthew chuckled and tilted his head toward the structure as they passed it while driving on the road. "Sandpiper Bay Lighthouse was built in 1820 and the lantern still works."

Riley recalled the articles she'd read because lighthouses fascinated her. "Is there a live-in caretaker?"

"Not really. It's a rental." Matthew dropped one hand from the wheel to rest on the tan leg of his uniform.

Minutes later they reached the police station. Matthew parked and they got out before the single-story stone building with windows on either side of a tall metal door. She opened the door for him and followed him inside. He had to be well over six feet and lanky.

The front half of the large space was partitioned from the back with a long reception desk. At seven forty, the place was quiet and dark without any lights on.

Matthew flipped a switch. Overhead fluorescent tracks flickered and then brightened. He tapped the reception desk.

"Nancy is a public service officer, POS, who manages the phones and our records. She's here Monday through Friday. Rosita, our part-timer, works Tuesday through Sunday from ten till four. She fills in wherever she's needed as a civilian officer."

"We used those in Phoenix, too." Civilians not sworn in but trained to do fingerprinting and other jobs that freed up the police to patrol. Even they had turned on her.

"Folks just love her—she took it upon herself to build a community outreach center. Nancy, Rosita, you, me, and of course the chief, makes five. Rosita was hoping for a full-time position, but it's just not in the budget."

Had she prevented Rosita getting a promotion? Riley might have yet another obstacle to overcome.

Matthew turned to the left and opened a door that led to the chief's office. "He comes in at eight. You and I are going to switch every two months as to who works nights, but I'll start since you're new."

"Thanks." She scanned the space for a hint about her boss. A picture of him and his wife, Shelley, a plump woman with a friendly smile, sat on the corner of his desk. A picture of twin baby girls in hospital blankets. Laptop, closed. A potted plant. Shelves crammed with police procedurals and books on the island. "Usually the new guy gets the awful shift."

"I like it actually. I've always been a night owl, so it suits me."

Riley nodded her appreciation.

Matthew shut the chief's door and they crossed the lobby to the right side of the building and opened another door. This led to three offices—one had a nameplate that read Riley Harper, the center one was for Matthew Sniders, and the last was labeled Rosita Sanchez.

"The kitchen and bathroom are at the very end of this hall. Our building stores the town records which is most of the containers in the rear half of the room. We have files going back to the eighteen hundreds."

"That's incredible."

"I think so too." Matthew opened the door to her office and flicked on the light. "Nancy put the nameplate up for you so that you'd feel welcome."

She'd have to thank her later. "That's really nice."

Matthew nodded. "She's a sweetheart. I'm sure you'll make the space your own. Within guidelines of course. Chief will no doubt load you up with paperwork."

She walked into the small office just big enough for a six-foot oak desk, an office chair, and two metal fold-out chairs against the wall, with a map of the island centered above. Shelves lined the side walls, and a clock hung behind her desk. It didn't have the correct time.

"Let me guess—this was storage?"

Matthew laughed and hooked his thumb over his belt buckle. "Maybe you should be a detective. What gave it away? This is the first time we've ever needed three offices at the station."

She pointed to the deep grooves in the beige carpet that didn't match the current shelves, indicating a file cabinet or something heavier. Old bracket holes from mesh shelving hadn't been filled in. It desperately needed a coat of paint, but she didn't dare say so and risk alienating her coworkers. Unless this was some kind of passive-aggressive protest to her being here?

She pulled her shoulders back and kept her feelings to herself.

I can do anything for a year.

A bell chimed and Matthew turned toward the lobby which was visible from her office if the interior door was open. "There's the chief now." He lifted his hand.

Chief Bradley Barnes smiled shortly. His dark-blue suit stretched across his middle and shoulders. Thick but not fat—as if he'd once played football. He emanated strength.

"Morning," she said.

"Sniders showed you around?" The tone was gruff. Polite. She didn't feel comfortable bringing up his kindness yesterday in front of Matthew.

"He has, yes."

"Good. Give me ten minutes to get a cup of joe, and then meet me in my office to go over the paperwork. We'll get you keys to the place and the car." His tone was pleasant enough, but she cringed when he ducked into his office and slammed the door.

Matthew melted back toward the breakroom. "I'll get the coffee started. Nancy will be surprised. You okay?"

"Yes, thanks." Riley went into the space she was supposed to make her own, but it felt generic. She'd tossed a few personal items into her purse before work and now pulled out a photo of Kyra from eighth grade graduation and set it on her desk. Next to that she put her leather notebook and an engraved silver pen from her parents. Pretty barren, but she'd pick up a plant or two later. Surely she'd be given a desktop or a laptop?

She brought out her phone and took a seat on the chair. Immediately she realized a wheel was loose and the seat dipped. Riley smacked her elbow on the desk. "Ouch!"

Chief Barnes looked up from the lobby where he'd been perusing phone messages while standing over the desk.

Had the loose wheel been part of his "welcome" package?

She'd been razzed and vilified in Phoenix after the incident where she'd been forced to testify against a fellow officer. Rats had been stuffed in her patrol car—live ones. Her tires on her personal vehicle had been slashed. Traitor painted across the windshield.

This was child's play compared to what her old department had put her through.

She stood and picked up her notepad and pen to take to Chief Barnes's office.

"I'm ready to get started, sir."

"Have a seat."

By ten, Riley had a cramp in her fingers from signing so much paperwork. Insurance, contracts, and her initials on twenty-five pages of the Sandpiper Bay Police Force manual.

Chief Barnes pushed back from his desk and stood up. "Let's take a break, and then I'll drive you around the island. Show you around. We'll be back at one for lunch with everyone as a welcome to the team."

"That sounds nice." Riley patted her hollow stomach, grateful that her mother had made her breakfast this morning.

She walked to her office, passing a square-shouldered blonde who must be Nancy. The woman was on the phone and typing on a keyboard, her face to the monitor and not Riley.

Matthew was gone, and Rosita Sanchez's office was dark. Riley went out the front door, the weight of the keys to the building heavy in her pocket.

Chief Barnes was already in his SUV, so she climbed into the passenger side. She didn't see another sedan and wondered where her car was.

"Matthew took me past the lighthouse this morning. It sure is pretty."

"Every island in Maine has one. It was important in the fishing heyday." He checked his mirrors and reversed to the street. "Since Matthew already showed you that loop of the island, we'll head down Main Street."

Riley sat forward, excited to see businesses and homes where she would live for the next year. Sandpiper Bay had a good reputation for a tourist's dream holiday. Lobster and boating, fishing and hiking. There were a lot of national parks that were so different from Arizona.

"We're just at the end of our summer season. June, July, and August we have an average high of seventy-five degrees. Next week is September and it will be cooler in the mornings. It's been known to snow in October."

She'd never seen snow, and neither had Kyra. "Phoenix was having a heat wave, so this feels really great."

He chuckled and pointed out some restaurants. "The food here is better than average, if I say so myself. We pride ourselves on not having a single chain restaurant on the island."

"Not even a Mickey D's? My daughter might go through withdrawals." Riley was only partially kidding. "What can you tell me about the school situation?"

"She's fourteen?"

"Yes, and missing her first year of high school with her friends."

"Because of the significant snowfall and extreme conditions, we always have the option to study online. Homeschool. If the weather's good, Doreen Breckenridge runs classes at the schoolhouse next to the library. It's right over there." He pointed to a squat two-story building, near a three-story building painted in corals. "She was a principal for ten years in Bangor and semi-retired here when her husband did."

"Kyra's a bookworm, but I think she might miss being around other kids. I thought that she could study on the mainland?"

"Ferry doesn't run in a storm, which happens quite a bit in the winter."

"They don't run, at all? What if there's an emergency?"

"Then we get a phone call." He peered over the frames of his sunglasses at her. "That a problem?"

"No." She hoped not.

"You'll get to know everyone. We have a lot of good community activities for the full-timers."

"How many teenagers are there? Year-round?"

He stopped at a stop sign and waved to a young mom pushing a stroller.

"Hmm. The Petersons have Josh and Cindy—thirteen and sixteen? Then the Monroes have a daughter, fifteen. Yeah, I think Moira is fifteen. I can't remember all their names, but there's at least twenty freshmen to seniors. The K through eight had seventy-five."

"Total?" She sucked in a breath. Kyra's last class had forty kids and that was common.

"Yep. I see your face." He clucked his teeth. "I wish that when we were raising our girls in Portland that I'd had the chance to be here. It's low crime. Tight-knit. You can trust your neighbor."

There was no way Kyra was going to enjoy living here. Or her busy mom. For some reason she'd had it in her head that they'd be more...mobile. That they wouldn't be trapped on the island. That the ferry would still run during the worst of winter.

Her pulse sped. "But your wife wants to leave? Shelley?"

"Only because of the grandkids. She loves it here now too."

Riley exhaled and decided to deal with Kyra's reaction later.

"Low crime sounds perfect."

"We have our share of thefts and petty stuff but it's usually the tourists. Here we all know each other."

It sounded idyllic. Too good to be true.

They drove down another three miles. "See that forest of evergreen?"

She turned the way his finger pointed. "Yes."

"When we do have local trouble, it often happens around this area. Mackabee's Park."

"What does that mean?"

He slid his gaze from the cluster of trees—pines and fir, but mostly lovely evergreen with thick branches. "It's shortened from a Native American name nobody could pronounce."

She tried to hide her reaction to his crude observation. "What kind of trouble?"

"There was a shooting. A stabbing. People go a little crazy. The kids, teenagers especially, claim to see fairy lights." He lowered his voice. "Dark magic."

Riley's mouth dried. "What do you think?"

He chuckled but his lips firmed. "I don't believe in hocus pocus. I'll tell you, one officer to another, that strange things happen around Mackabee's Park. Just be aware. And keep your daughter away from the woods."

Chapter Four

Keep Kyra away from the woods?

Riley wasn't sure if this was another hazing for the new police officer in town or if Chief Barnes was serious. She couldn't dig deeper because Matthew Sniders called to say that lunch was ready.

Barnes turned around at the end of Main Street, pointing out various outbuildings used for boat repair or netting. He mentioned the good work Rosita was doing at the library with her outreach. Nothing sinister. No warnings.

Her beliefs were broader than simple black and white. She believed that there was more to the world than what you could see or feel with your five senses. As an officer of the law, she gave precedence to hard facts.

The chief cleared his throat and she turned from where she'd been gazing out the window. "If you like seafood there are numerous places I can recommend. We also have two Chinese food options, but they're pickup only."

"That's great to hear. I'll tell Kyra *after* I let her down about the golden arches."

Barnes chuckled. "We just passed a restaurant that has the best pizza known to man. Piazza Piper. The garlic rolls and mozzarella sticks are unbelievable." He patted his middle as he drove.

"Pizza is a family favorite."

"On the island, the Sandpiper Bay dish is lobster rolls, if you're looking for comfort food."

"I've never had one."

"Try the Lobster Pot. You'll thank me."

The loop had taken less than an hour and by noon they were back at the station. The chief parked in the back next to a tiny two-door Fiat in cobalt blue.

"There you are," he said, pointing to the car.

"What do you mean?" She frowned and studied his face. He wore a neutral expression, but she could see him fight to maintain it. Was this another joke? Everyone on the island had a lousy sense of humor.

"That's for you to drive, personal and while on duty. No drinking and driving. Nobody else but you can drive the car. You remember the paperwork."

She would have remembered a description of the car but there hadn't been one. No drinking and driving, that was a no-brainer. "A Fiat? In the snow?"

"Great tires and traction. Hard to believe, but it's true. No mountains here to worry about, so it should do nicely. We have a limit to the amount of cars allowed on the island. Not just because the island is small but to protect the integrity of our environment."

He patted the dash of his sturdy SUV.

She leaned backward against her car door. "You're serious?"

"We did a lot of research before purchasing this vehicle. It's only a year old. Truth was, it also fit our budget. Your salary isn't cheap." He raised a shoulder.

She longed to tell him that she'd taken a pay cut to work here, but it would only be a reminder as to why she'd needed the job.

Exhaling, Riley climbed out of the SUV and shut the door with a tad more force than necessary.

He rubbed his jaw to hide his mouth.

He was tickled by her reaction. She decided then and there to buck up and not give him anything more to laugh about.

Riley met him by the back door, eye to eye.

His smirk faded. "What are you doing?"

"I just need to clear the air." She braced her shoulders to stand up for herself. "I have a feeling you don't want me here." Maybe he'd wanted the budget to hire Rosita full time?

He shrugged and gave her a straight look. "I didn't want another officer at the station. My boss decided differently."

Riley held his gaze. "But I'm here. All I want is acceptance."

"That's difficult. If my boss wanted another officer in this station, I should have some say in the matter." A muscle in his cheek twitched. "You wouldn't be here now."

"I'm a good officer. And if you give me time, I'll—"

He interrupted. "You'll what? Prove it? You have a bad rep as someone who isn't loyal. We are a team here. I don't know that you'll fit."

Her belly tightened but she wouldn't show him that his words stung. She'd heard worse before now.

"You saw my file in field performance. My test scores. I am more than capable of doing this job."

"More than capable isn't enough. *You don't* belong here."

Riley stepped back as if slapped. "The contract has been signed. I don't quit. I don't give up."

Chief Barnes glared at her with cold eyes. "Let's see how you do this winter." He heaved a sigh. "I can make it as hard on you as I want. Got a feeling you'll be paying me, and then we can get the next guy a real car."

Fuming, Riley followed her boss inside to the breakroom where Matthew Sniders was putting hoagies on a platter. Nancy set out a bowl of chips. A dark-haired woman with a curvy figure packed into black slacks and a button-up blouse pulled paper plates from a cupboard.

"We're here," the chief said as if the confrontation outside hadn't happened.

From the way Matthew darted glances her way, she knew they'd all heard it.

The dark-haired woman lifted her head with a forced smile. "Hi. I'm Rosita. Welcome to Sandpiper Bay Police Department."

Swallowing her pride, Riley shook Rosita's hand. "Riley Harper. Thanks."

The statuesque blonde greeted Riley next. "We didn't officially meet. Nancy Winston."

"Hi."

"We thought this might be a nice way to get to know one another," she said into the awkward moment.

Like so many things in her life lately, Riley brazened her way through the tension-filled lunch.

At four thirty when she was allowed to leave, she said polite goodbyes. Unless the chief had an attitude change, the year was going to be pure hell.

When she arrived home to the rental cabin, her mom and Kyra were on the back porch with iced tea and a veggie tray, the two chatting as they looked out at the water.

"Mom!" Kyra called in welcome. "Just in time for dinner. Lobster? Please? We can take the car."

Riley bit her tongue and made herself smile warmly. This was important. This mattered. Family. Not some jackass police chief who thought he could judge her.

"And hello to you too! Can I run upstairs and change out of this uniform?" She believed in what it stood for but today it weighed heavy.

"I'll pour you a glass of wine," her mom called as Riley ran up the stairs.

"Thanks." Riley quickly changed into a Henley with jeans. Though not yet five it would be dark soon. After the verbal beating she'd taken, she wasn't in the mood to go out, but would make the effort.

When she came downstairs, her mom and Kyra were in the kitchen. Her daughter's smile made her happy. She decided not to bring up the creepy woods or the mean chief. It was best to separate her job from her family.

Riley thought she'd be able to do that before but people, other officers, had made it personal. Impossible to ignore.

"What did you two do today?" She hardly recognized her perky voice.

"Mom, we biked all over the island. I'm starting to think this place doesn't stink quite so much. Sammy is totes jealous, but I told her she can visit. Can she?"

"Of course!" Definitely not the time to share about no fast-food restaurants. The island would be back on the black list. "I'll check with her mom."

Samantha Perez was her daughter's best friend...just as shy as Kyra. Sammy's parents were friends with Riley's ex, which made things hard sometimes. Fraser Harper hadn't been a good husband or a good father. Drinking changed his temperament, and she was never sure which man would be waiting for her when she got home.

The good Fraser was fun and loving. The bad Fraser had broken Kyra's arm. Riley had handed him divorce papers the next day and moved them out of the family home, buying a smaller three-bedroom just for her and Kyra. Her daughter came first. Always.

Riley accepted the white wine her mom handed her. "Mom, what did you think of the island?"

"It's lovely. We passed a library and saw a lighthouse. And an Italian restaurant overlooking the water."

"I think everything overlooks the water," Kyra said.

"You might be right." Riley sipped and leaned back against the kitchen counter. "I feel like we're on vacation. If only I didn't have to go to work."

Kyra laughed. "I know. Me too. We stopped at the library and bought a few DVDs from this decade. Cheap."

"That's good—more romance?"

"Comedy, Mom. Rom-coms are the best."

"I bought a few used books on sale too," Susan said. "But we need to get baskets for the bikes."

"We can do that." Riley set the glass down. "I wonder if they sell them at the market."

"If not, they can order it." Susan eyed the still-full glass. "How was your day, Riley?"

"It was long. Uncomfortable." Learning and *accepting* that she couldn't outrun her past. She'd have to prove herself to these people. But how?

She gave the ceiling an eye roll. Riley wasn't much for religion, but she believed in a higher power. Something for the greater good.

"If we want to go out to dinner, my contract says I can't have even one drink and drive the company car. Nobody else can drive it either."

Her mom's brow lifted.

Kyra scrunched her nose. "Weird."

She shrugged and played by the rules. "Not a big deal. You feel like having seafood or Italian?"

"Lobster!" her family said in unison.

"All right. Grab your purses, ladies, and whatever you do, don't laugh at the car."

Kyra's joy fled as she got a peek at the new wheels, but she didn't gripe as she folded herself into the back seat. Her knees were to her chest.

Her mom got into the passenger seat, her chest shaking with silent laughter. "Oh, Riley."

Riley glanced at her mother, then started the engine. "You have no idea, Mom."

At that comment Susan studied Riley with comprehension and she knew that her mom realized it had been an awful day.

Susan's hand briefly covered hers. "We saw the lighthouse on our bike ride."

"The librarian said that the top part is open to the public," Kyra piped up from the back.

"Matthew Sniders, another officer at the station, told me that it's a rental."

"The bottom half?" Kyra suggested. "I want to see it. The light is supposed to still work on foggy nights to save the ships from crashing into the island."

"I'd enjoy seeing it too. I already have my schedule so let's make plans to explore. Days for the next two months, then Officer Sniders and I will switch."

Susan placed her purse at her feet. "I don't imagine much bad happens here, so night shift probably isn't terrible. I used to worry about you in Phoenix."

"Me too, Mom. I think Nana's right about this being a safer place."

Riley smiled at her daughter from the rearview mirror. It meant a lot that she was willing to give Sandpiper Bay a chance.

After a short drive they arrived at the Lobster Pot and nabbed a parking spot near the entrance. It was less than a mile from their home, so if they wanted to walk they could—during the nicer months anyway.

The three of them had to climb out of the Fiat like a bunch of clowns. She was not amused, preferring dignity over a comedy act. She had to suck it up—it might be insulting but she didn't want to give the chief an opportunity to win his bet.

There was no one to seat them so they took a table next to a thick plexiglass window where they could watch the sun go down.

"The librarian told us that our warm days are almost gone," Kyra said. "I used to complain all the time that it was too hot."

"Remember those words." Riley laughed.

"It's pretty here now, but I wonder how dismal it will be in the dead of winter." Kyra sighed. Was there anything more dramatic than a teenage girl?

Susan patted Kyra's shoulder. "We have each other and that's what counts."

"Hi! Welcome to the Lobster Pot. I'm Katie." The bubbly young woman had shoulder-length springy black curls and bright-blue eyes. "What can I get you?"

Riley nodded at Kyra who burst out, "We all want the lobster."

Katie grinned and tucked her hands into an apron around her waist. "Of course you do. Is this your first visit to the island?"

"We just moved here," her mom said. "I'm Susan. This hungry miss is Kyra, and my daughter is Riley Harper, the new police officer in town."

Katie beamed at them all with a welcoming smile. "Well then, welcome to our restaurant and Sandpiper Bay. I'm tickled that you came here tonight. We'll have to leave you with a good impression—we're known for the best lobster dinners."

"Chief Barnes said as much. None of us have ever had it, so if it tastes as good as it looks, you're halfway there." Riley enjoyed the warm welcome after the cold reception earlier in the day.

"It will. Absolutely." She giggled, and Riley guessed her to be in her twenties. "I own this place with my boyfriend, Carter. He's cooking."

"Is it clumsy to eat? Do we need one of those bibs?" Kyra gestured to the other diners.

Katie gave her a wink. "Not for the three of you. I'll have Carter crack the lobster so it won't be so hard to eat. Later, when you're pros, you can crack it yourself."

"That would be wonderful!" Riley felt immense relief to be guided through their first time eating lobster.

Katie took their beverage orders and hurried off. The restaurant had about a dozen diners, leaving half the tables empty. This building was two stories. So far the tallest structure, other than the lighthouses, had been the library at three stories tall. It must have to do with the winter storms.

Katie returned with two glasses of iced tea and a coke for Kyra. A few minutes later she dropped off plastic bibs and a dish of metal lobster crackers which resembled a nutcracker. "You probably won't need these, but I'll leave it just in case."

"Well, this is very nice, isn't it?" Susan looked around with approval. "What a lovely girl."

"I like her," Kyra said, sipping her drink through a straw.

"So do I." For the first time that day Riley felt relaxed and pampered. The knot in her stomach after the unpleasant encounter with her boss had miraculously disappeared.

"Here you are." Katie brought out one plate at a time, with the sides of corn and sourdough bread. "Don't be afraid to get messy." She dropped a handful of the plastic packets of wipes in the center of the table. "We've got plenty more, don't worry. And two large sinks in the restroom if these don't do the trick."

"I'm so excited," Kyra said, her green eyes sparkling. "It looks amazing."

Since the lobsters had been cracked open for them, they were able to dive right in. The meat was delicious—soft and rich and dipped in lemon butter, it was a taste of heaven. Riley moaned with pleasure. Kyra ate hers in record-breaking time, then looked at their still-full plates.

Nana shook her head. "No way, Kyra. You have your corn and all that yummy warm bread. I'm not going to feel the slightest ounce of guilt devouring every tiny bite." But of course, she relented and gave her granddaughter a claw.

"Thanks, Nana!"

True happiness warmed her from the inside out as she watched her family enjoy themselves. She prayed that this island would be the respite they all needed and deserved.

Katie made them a to-go package shaped like a swan filled with garlic bread. She added a quart of lobster bisque. "No charge. Thanks for choosing us, and please don't be strangers."

"How about every day?" Kyra asked hopefully.

"If you show up daily, I'll put you to work. How old are you, love?"

"Fourteen."

"Wait until you're sixteen, and then I'll give you a job."

Kyra frowned as the teasing took a turn. "We'll be long gone by then. One year, right, Mom?"

"That's the plan." If she didn't get fired first.

When they got home, Kyra stomped into the room she'd staked out for herself on the ground floor, behind the kitchen. She blared her music.

"Now what did I do?" Riley downed the glass of white wine on the counter while her mom put away the food. "I can't do anything right for her."

"That's a teenager for you." Susan clapped her hand over Riley's knuckles. "All those hormones out of whack. Remember what it was like?"

"I know, but we had such a nice dinner."

"I think she just got carried away having a good time and she needed to remind you that she wasn't happy. That's all. It'll be better when she can go to school again."

"Buckle up, Mom." She added more wine to her glass and poured one for her mother. "Things got worse."

"I'm afraid to ask."

"I found out today that the ferry doesn't run in the worst of winter, which means homeschooling. Not something I even thought to ask because it is so far out of our norm."

Susan's eyes widened. "What do they expect us to do?"

"It's online. They have their normal curriculum and right here they have a retired high school teacher who helps students who need it."

"Oh, dear. That leaves very little socializing. But it seems the way of the world these days. Even my book club from Phoenix meets online."

"It's sad, isn't it?" She sipped her wine.

Her mom looked her in the eye. "Tough day?"

"Chief doesn't want me here. He's aware of my history and doesn't trust me."

"Give him time and he'll warm up to you. You told the truth when you testified against that officer."

"I had no choice, as you know."

"It shows character to go against the pack. You did the right thing."

Riley pressed her hand to her aching heart. "So why does it feel so bad?"

Chapter Five

The following morning Riley arrived at the station just as Matthew pulled in. She couldn't help but notice that her Fiat was about a third the size of his sedan. She hadn't expected a parade on her arrival, but the chief's treatment of her so far was less than stellar. Nothing overt enough to get him fired or written up, just...rude. She'd gotten good at focusing on her job and tuning out the rest. It saddened her that she'd have to do that here too.

Matthew waited by the front door, holding it open for her.

"Morning!" She passed him into the building. At seven thirty, it was still dark as Nancy didn't come in until eight. "You're here early. When do you switch to nights?"

"Tonight." Matthew smoothed back his ginger hair that he'd styled with gel. "I was already up and had some paperwork to finish. I'll head out around noon to sleep."

Not everyone was rude, and she'd remember that. "I appreciate you letting me get acclimatized to the island first."

Matthew flicked on the overhead lights. "No worries. So, how was your second night in Sandpiper? Did you try out one of our restaurants? You can't get fresher fish."

"We sure did! We had the most amazing lobster dinner and the owners treated us very nice. Got home around seven, and once my daughter decided to behave like a human being again, she joined us for a romping game of Scrabble."

"Never did like that game much." He stepped to the right, toward their offices. "Which restaurant?"

"The Lobster Pot. Since we're not familiar with dissecting a whole lobster, Katie had her boyfriend Carter crack them for us. They were so good, all three of us gobbled it up!"

He stopped before her office. "You never had lobster before? I grew up on the stuff. Lobster rolls, lobster mac and cheese, lobster bisque..."

"No wonder you stayed." She grinned. "My ex and I were big beef eaters—give us a prime rib or a beef tenderloin and we were in heaven."

"I've never known anyone who doesn't love seafood." His brow arched in disbelief.

"I do! I mean, shrimp and fish. And now lobster. It was as big as our plates. And lemon butter? Garlic bread?" She patted her stomach.

He rocked back on his heels, hands at his hips. "Glad you enjoyed it. If you didn't, this island would be a tough sell."

Riley laughed, liking Matthew and feeling comfortable with him. She hoped he'd be an ally. If Chief Barnes thought he could demean her to the point that she'd leave with her head between her knees, he was mistaken.

"Tell me about yourself, Matthew. What do you do for entertainment around here?"

"Depends on the day—there's always something going on. I have my own lobster pot offshore and I take my dinghy out every other day. If I snare one, it ends up as dinner. I've got a crab trap as well."

"Tough life," she teased. She opened the door to her office and turned on the switch. "How do local islanders spend their time?"

"A good portion of those that stay year-round own businesses." He shrugged. "You'll want to meet them, I'm sure."

"I plan on dropping into as many places as I can to introduce myself. Phoenix was too big to do that. What else is there?"

"Karaoke every Tuesday and Friday at The Shack."

"Do you sing?" She kept one eye on the door in case the chief showed up and caught them chatting instead of working.

"Nah. I go to have a few beers and check out the pretty ladies." His throat flushed. "It's got the best fish and chips in town. Heck, I bet it beats anyplace on the mainland too."

"I met Coby the first day we arrived on the ferry and he told me the same. I figured he was bragging, but if you agree, we'll have to give them a try."

"Watch him," Matthew warned, his hand on the knob. "He's popular with the ladies."

Too charming, as she'd thought. "Yeah. I caught that. So. Karaoke, eating, and fishing to fill up our free time."

He chuckled. "There are a lot of national parks around here that you can spend the day at if you go off-island. The many lighthouses."

She kept her gaze on Matthew as she said, "The chief drove me past Mackabee's Park yesterday." Would he mention any odd happenings?

Matthew stilled. "There are some decent trails in the trees—nothing too strenuous."

"Is it dangerous? The chief suggested..."

"No! It's just a park." Matthew fidgeted and ducked into his office. "Gotta get this paperwork done."

Matthew had just acted very strange. What was it with the woods?

The front entrance chimed and Nancy entered. She wore navy-blue slacks and a white SBPD polo. The chief, in a dark-gray suit, followed her in. They were laughing but stopped when they saw Riley standing there.

Not giving her boss a chance to spoil her mood, she spoke first. "Good morning, Chief. Nancy. It's a beautiful day, isn't it?"

"It'll be better with coffee," Barnes snapped. "You get that ready yet? Since you're here early and all."

"No, Chief. I signed about a million papers yesterday but didn't see that on my job description."

"That right?" His dark-brown eyes narrowed. "You think you're too good to make coffee?"

"Of course not." Her cheeks burned.

"No need to get into a huff about it. I always make the coffee," Nancy interjected with a smile at Riley and then Barnes. The tall blonde patted Riley's arm in passing and headed for the kitchen.

"If you'd like me to make coffee tomorrow, I'm happy to do it," she told Barnes. "I'm a team player."

"Not what I heard. I had a nice long chat with some officers in your previous precinct. Nobody had a good word to say."

"Must have spoken with the wrong department. I was in the Cactus Park Precinct." She pasted on a sweet smile to hide her bluff. Truth was, they all considered her a rat.

"I'm fully aware of where you used to work before you were fired."

"I wasn't fired, Chief. They had no grounds to let me go." She raised her chin. "I was on an extended leave of absence when I accepted the position here."

"You quit."

"To transfer here. My record was exemplary for fifteen years before that." She lifted her shoulders and held his gaze. "Honesty isn't always the best policy."

Heavy silence stretched between them.

At last Barnes said, "I want you to drive around the island today. Go meet people. Make sure they know who you are."

In other words, stay out of his sight. She could do that. "Yes, sir."

"We don't have much crime on the island. I don't know why my boss was so insistent on hiring *you*."

"I am here to stay, Chief."

"We'll see about that. Some folks go crazy during the winter months, did you know that? Get claustrophobic from being trapped."

Her stomach tightened. "That won't happen to me."

"You never know." He went into his office and slammed the door.

Riley hustled down the hall to the kitchen for a cup of coffee to go. Neither Matthew nor Nancy spoke to her, but they shot sympathetic glances her way.

Didn't matter what they thought. No one could hurt her anymore. Not her ex-husband, not the lies and rumors that had spread like wildfire through her old precinct, fanned by "the club" of men who befriended her partner, an officer who shot a suspect in cold blood.

She'd built a protective seal around her heart and the only person who could make it ache was Kyra. Because she loved her so very much, and her happiness was more important than her own.

Nancy opened a box of donuts and offered it to Riley. "Have something to eat before you go out meeting all those new people." She leaned in. "Don't mind him, he's not getting enough at home."

Matthew spurted his coffee, and Riley gave a surprised laugh. So far, Chief Barnes was the only person who outwardly disliked her. Maybe Rosita.

"Did I take Rosita's place?" Riley chose a sugar glazed donut.

Nancy helped herself to three donuts on a small plate. "She was hopeful, but a position wasn't ever promised."

Riley nodded. "I wonder why, if the budget is so tight for Sandpiper Bay, they wanted another full-time officer?"

"Our crime rate has gone up a bit compared to previous years, as has our population. Ten percent across the board." Matthew sipped his coffee. "Rosita is great, but she's not licensed to carry a weapon. She can't arrest anyone. Another officer was needed here. There weren't many applicants, and none with your experience."

"I see." She would prove herself and do things by the book. Topping off her to-go cup, Riley wished the others a good day and headed out the back to avoid another run-in with the boss. Whatever his problem with her was, he'd have to suck it up, because she was here for a year as stated in the contract.

She placed her coffee in the cup holder of the Fiat and started the engine, honking twice before leaving the lot. "Can't keep a good woman down."

Since she planned on doing the whole loop, Riley decided to start at the ferry depot and work her way toward Mackabee's Park and around until she ended up back at the depot.

Colorful homes and businesses had a seaside feel with pelicans, dolphins, and lobster figures on everything from mailboxes to murals. The depot was plain in comparison but sturdy to withstand the gusts from the harbor.

She parked on the street where the man with the chicken lived, but the porch and rocking chair were empty. The street had light traffic, mostly pedestrians since the ferry had recently docked, so she strode across the road.

Riley studied her reflection in the glass window of the building where you could purchase tickets or passes for the ferry. Tan uniform with short sleeves,

Kevlar vest with a radio, baton, and spray. Cuffs. Gun in her holster. Hair in a bun. Mirrored sunglasses. Riley was an officer of the law just as she'd always dreamed. Other girls had played with dolls, but she'd liked to play cops and robbers. After what had happened in Phoenix, she'd almost turned in her badge, but that would have let the bad guys win.

The door pushed open and a young man hurried out. Deke. Coby had pointed him out as a man who knew everyone.

"Morning!" she called as he passed by.

Deke turned with a questioning smile. "Hi." His brow furrowed, causing a silver hoop in the left one to flash, and he scraped his hand through his longish brown hair. "Oh! You must be the new cop Coby was talking about."

"I am. Officer Harper." She held out her hand. Coby seemed to be the island gossip.

Deke shook it. His hands were calloused from hard work, his muscles bulky at the biceps and shoulders. He was no stranger to manual labor, but he seemed to like it. "Deke Anderson."

"Is Captain Wyatt in? I was hoping to meet him." She gestured to the depot behind her.

"Yeah, he's—"

A man's voice called out, "My hat!"

Riley whirled toward a trio of guys in their early twenties waiting around the luggage area. A seagull had a Giants cap by the bill and swept it toward the harbor.

Deke laughed. "The gulls are scavengers, man."

The other two men, one in a black knit cap, one with bleached hair, teased their buddy, who looked flustered. "That was my favorite hat!"

She grinned at them. "Want to file a report? I've never arrested a seagull."

"Do they even have seagulls in Phoenix?" Deke asked.

Laughing, she said, "Not that I've seen." Boy, gossip really did spread fast here.

The guys picked up their bulky backpacks and slung them over their shoulders. The man with the missing cap said, "Guess I get to buy a new hat. That's one way to never forget Sandpiper Bay."

"Officer, do you know how far it is to Mackabee's Park?" The man with bleached hair glared at the seagulls. "We're walking."

"I don't, sorry. I'm new to the area." Riley looked at Deke, who didn't seem worried or concerned that they'd be going to the forest. Barnes had to be hazing her.

Deke hooked a thumb to his left. "Head down this road to Main Street and you can catch a trolley to the park. It'll save you five miles."

"Thanks!" Stolen Hat Man said.

"Nice to meet you, Officer Harper," Deke said. "Take it easy, guys." He strode toward Fifth Street where she'd passed a market and a diner. The other men ambled off.

Riley popped into the depot, but the captain was inundated with customers. Checking the time, she decided to come back when it wasn't as busy and selected a map from the brochure rack.

If she went right from the ferry dock, she'd eventually reach her cabin. She walked to the street and looked to her left. The narrow road followed the water but there were no other buildings. Assorted vendors worked beneath colorful canopies.

Curious as to what they sold, Riley walked toward them until she reached an older woman in a chair working on needlepoint, surrounded by tubs of shells and handcrafted baskets.

"Hello," she said.

The brown-skinned, wrinkled elder looked up from her project. "Well, hello yourself, Officer. Can I interest you in a hand-embroidered scarf or perhaps a basket to hold your trinkets?"

"Neither today. I'm new to the island and figured I'd introduce myself to the locals. Officer Harper. I'm from Phoenix."

"That right?" She spat out some chewing tobacco. "I'm Melo. From Mexico City—we used to be neighbors, and now are again."

"It's a small world." Riley admired the exquisite handiwork on a basket that might fit one of the bikes. "I've changed my mind. I'd like this, please."

It was wicker and if it didn't work for groceries, they could use it indoors for books or blankets near the hearth.

"That'll be twenty dollars." Melo wrapped the basket in brown paper.

Riley pulled out her wallet and handed the twenty over. "Thank you so much."

"Come see me again, Officer Harper. Good day to you!" Melo returned to her chair and her needlepoint.

Riley left the canopy and headed toward the next one. She recognized the trio of guys from the ferry. The one who'd needed a hat was trying on new caps, as two young women flirted with them.

Their voices carried. "I'm Lacey," the blonde said, "and this is my friend, Chloe." Chloe was a shorter redhead. "We're here for a couple of days. What about you, cuties?"

Black Knit Cap Guy said, "We're here for the weekend."

Riley noticed a thick accent similar to Matthew's. The friends must be from somewhere close.

"Where ya staying?" Lacey rubbed her arm against the one trying on hats.

"We're going to camp in Mackabee's Park." He nodded at his backpack. "We've got our camping gear and some special cameras. Do you know anything about the woods? We hear there was some crazy shit going on. Like paranormal hunters weird."

All three guys laughed nervously.

Riley listened closer.

"Cool," Chloe said.

"I lived here years ago," Lacey told them with a saucy smile. "You don't want to mess around in those woods." She made claws out of her hands. "Or something might eat you up!"

"You lived here? That's awesome!" Bleached blond guy scooted next to Lacey. "You ever see anything?"

"I tell you what—why don't you come on by my cabin later, maybe with some party supplies, and I'll tell you some stories you won't believe."

The guy trying on hats shook his head at his friend in the black knit cap. Lacey saw the move and gave a harsh laugh.

"Well, if you change your minds, come find me. We love to have a good time, don't we, Chloe?" She rattled off the address and hooked her arm in Chloe's. "See ya, suckers."

The blonde tossed her hair off her shoulder, revealing a snake tattoo on her neck. The redhead also had a hard look about her. The girls wore tank tops, no bras. Lacey's arms were covered in tattoos. It was sad to say that she'd met their kind in Phoenix. Riley hadn't expected to run into that seedy element here.

The duo crossed the street and headed toward The Shack. Looking for trouble, and they'd probably find it. Riley could ask Coby later, seeing as he seemed to be gossip central.

The guys joked around about the two girls, but they weren't interested. Nope, they were talking about the haunted woods. The guy who'd lost his Giants cap to the gull bought a Sandpiper Bay hat and pulled it low over his face. They continued on toward Main Street and the trolley.

What was it about the woods? Riley needed to get to the bottom of this. Would Matthew tell her more? Or Coby? Barnes wasn't hazing her... Other people knew stories about the forest being haunted.

Riley bought a bottle of water from one of the street vendors and pulled out her map from the ferry depot. Her stomach rumbled and she regretted not taking a couple of donut holes with her.

She wasn't ready to return to the station. She needed to carry on. Find friends and find food. The two sort of went together. And man, could she ever use a friend.

Chapter Six

Riley read the colorful cartoon map of Sandpiper Bay. "Bake and Shake Bakery," she read aloud. She sniffed and breathed in vanilla. Chocolate. Sure enough, off the main road and around the corner was a two-story white and blue stone building. The awning covered chairs and tables in a matching blue. Various blooming plants in a riot of colors clustered in clay pots under the framed window.

As lovely as the shop was, the heavenly scents coming from within made her mouth water. It smelled so divine that thoughts of the donuts were history. Please be open, she said to herself, turning the handle on the white door. It twisted and she stepped inside, smiling as she reached the counter.

"Good morning," a pleasant female called out. The woman was pulling out a rack of cinnamon buns and small individual quiche pies which she put on a side counter to cool.

When she turned, Riley took in everything about her appearance at once. A middle-aged woman with a gray bun and plump red cheeks, smiling brown eyes, and an apron over a blue tee. Bake and Shake adorned the top in script font as though the individual strokes had been painted on.

"Hello. I could smell this bakery half a block away. Please tell me you're open for business." She checked the time on her cell phone. Nine. "There's nobody out front."

"You missed our six to eight thirty rush! Biz will pick up again in an hour."

"My lucky day!" She slipped the bag with her basket in it over her shoulder. "I'm the new police officer in town. Riley Harper. It's a delight to meet you..."

"Joan Higgins. Welcome! My husband Charlie is the baker."

"Everything smells amazing. Would do you recommend?" Sweat trickled down the back of Riley's uniform from the heat of the ovens. No wonder they had tables on the sidewalk.

"I'd heard that we were getting a new police officer. Well, let me give you a sample of our most popular morning items. Anything you don't care for?"

"Unfortunately, I love it all. Do you mind if I sit inside here and visit while I eat?"

"Not at all. I'll join you in the lull!" Joan slid a slice of quiche and a warm gooey bun on a plate, then made one for herself. "Here you go. The bad thing about owning a bakery is that I can't resist eating what comes out of the oven."

Riley laughed as she took her plate. "The name for that is the Taster. You have to be sure that it's suitable to be served."

"I like that. Charlie will get a kick out of it." They sat at one of the small tables lined up along the white stucco wall.

"So, welcome to Sandpiper Bay, Riley. Are you here on your own? Did your husband accompany you? Children?"

"No husband. My wonderful mother and my fourteen-year-old daughter are here with me." She didn't mention the year-long contract or that Kyra hadn't wanted to come.

"You must bring them around sometime," Joan said sincerely. "I'd love to meet them. I have a granddaughter around your daughter's age."

"That would be great. It will help Kyra to fit in once she makes new friends. Fourteen is a tough age." Riley sliced a piece of the warm quiche and took a bite. "Oh, Joan. This is so good!"

Joan had already eaten half of hers. "I know. Right?"

Riley had to laugh. "My mom is going to adore you."

"Even better." Joan dotted her mouth with a paper napkin. "Sorry, would you like coffee or tea? I was so hungry I forgot to offer."

"I have water, but thanks." She uncapped the bottle she'd bought from the vendor and sipped.

Joan cut a piece off her cinnamon bun and took a large bite. Riley noticed how her big brown eyes lit up as she ate—a woman who loved food and knew it was one of life's simple pleasures.

Riley finished her quiche. "So, I'm following the map of the island, hoping to meet the business owners. Any hidden treasures I should know about?"

"Hmm." Joan put down her fork and got up to retrieve a cold bottle of water from the cooler by the register. It had to be twenty degrees warmer inside the bakery.

Taking her seat again, Joan murmured, "Hidden treasures. Well, let's see. You have to check out the fishing harbor; it's on the opposite side of the island from the ferry."

"Okay. Why is that?"

"The plentiful fish, crab, and lobster is our daily bread, though it might be fancy and expensive in other parts of the world." Joan picked up her fork again. "The people here are the most genuine and caring folks I've ever met. No pretense. They don't judge a person for their personal belongings, but on character alone."

"That is a rare quality. I hope living here will teach Kyra, my daughter, how the world ought to be. She's at a vulnerable time in her life, trying to make sense of things. Right and wrong." Riley prayed the decisions she'd made would light the path for Kyra, but it was muddled. "I hope she'll have a better chance here."

"I bet it will be good for her, away from all the temptations of the city. Where are you from?"

"Phoenix, Arizona."

"Ah. Like night and day. Not that we don't have a little mischief going on once in a while, but it gives us old folks something to talk about." Joan smiled and polished off her cinnamon roll. "Finish eating, and I'll compile a list of important places and people for you to meet."

Twenty minutes later, Riley left the charming little bakery and headed down the street to a friend of Joan's who was a seamstress name Miriam Cramer. Miriam's husband was a carpenter. Together they supplied the furnishings for the boat builders, in addition to having independent clients.

Riley was getting an idea of how the island worked and how they survived the winter months without ever leaving. Everyone had at least one skill and was part of a network.

Three blocks down and a turn to the right she found the gray and white building, again a two-story. Homey curtains and a flower pot on the second-floor windowsill made her wonder if the owners lived above their shops. That would make perfect sense.

An OPEN sign was the only indication that a business was run inside. The locals would all know, so no need to explain their professions. Riley knocked gently once, then opened the small door which had tingling bells, letting the owners know they had company.

A thin woman sat facing the wall, working at a desk table with an old-fashioned sewing machine. It made a humming sound as she placed beautiful fabric onto the cover plate.

"Hello? Mrs. Cramer?" The lady never turned around. Joan had warned her that Miriam was hard of hearing.

Making noise so Miriam wouldn't be alarmed, Riley stomped her feet as she made her way to the woman's side.

"Hello, Mrs. Cramer. I'm Riley, a friend of Joan's."

The woman huffed and didn't look up. "No need to shout. I heard you straight off, but I was working on something. Guess I'm not anymore." She lifted her hand and finally turned around to Riley with a scowl.

Not the same warm personality as Joan Higgins. "I'm sorry to interrupt your work, Mrs. Cramer. I'm Riley Harper, new to the Sandpiper Bay Police Department."

"That's no job for a woman."

Riley bit the inside of her cheek and counted to five before answering. "I worked in Phoenix for almost fifteen years so I think I can handle whatever this island throws my way." So far, she hadn't seen anybody so much as litter.

"Good for you." A smile hovered over her wrinkled lips. "If you want clothes, that's what I've been doing for *forty* years. Wool coats, tailored slacks, blouses."

"Yes, ma'am. Joan said your products are better than buying something from the mainland."

"Everything on the island is better than the mainland," she scoffed. "Well, next time you're in the neighborhood, come on in. Don't be a stranger." Miriam turned back to her sewing. Riley had been dismissed.

She chuckled as she left the sewing shop, wondering if Joan had played a little joke on her. Or maybe come winter she might be grateful and put Miriam to work. Their winter clothes from Phoenix might not be warm enough.

Riley matched Joan's list with the map from the depot. She passed several restaurants that she was keen to visit, but she'd wait until her mom and Kyra were with her. Not only did she enjoy their company, but they deserved to experience the best this place had to offer.

She introduced herself to the man who ran the market, the woman who managed the ice cream shop, and the man in charge of the gas station. There were three souvenir shops that were doing a booming business, so she decided to check back later. She reached the marina that Joan had recommended. There was an array of tourists on this Friday morning, well, now close to noon.

Heading across the street, Riley watched several fishermen unloading their haul. Pleasure boats were also tied up on the wharf. The fish shop had black and red shingles and was much larger than she'd imagined. One side was strictly for the fishing crowd and sold live bait, a row of various fishing rods, wet suits, life jackets, and more. Several men purchased lunch boxes to take onboard.

A man that had to be Bernie Murphy with his shock of brilliant red hair and matching red beard helped the men unload their fish, then ran inside to take care of those who were shopping.

There was a woman at the cash register, in the second half of the rambling structure. She offered her hand in between customers. "Hi. I'm Riley Harper, the new police officer in town."

"I'm Sally Murphy! Welcome to the island."

"Just wanted to pop in and introduce myself. Joan Higgins mentioned your name. Said I couldn't miss Bernie's red hair and she was right."

"Ahh, so you found our wonderful Bake and Shake bakery? Us locals like to keep it secret from the day travelers. We worry that they'll buy everything in sight, and there will be nothing left for us. Can't blame them though. It's all so darn good."

"It is! Especially the quiche."

The woman put a hand over her mouth, her eyes bright. "I'm sorry, I got carried away. Usually Bernie's the chatty one."

Riley relaxed against the counter, her feet starting to hurt in her boots. It had been months since she'd been so active. "You're so busy that I won't keep you. Everyone's been so friendly." Except her boss, but that was her business.

"It comes naturally for most folks here. We enjoy seeing new faces and the tourists' excitement over the whales and the lighthouse and the lobster. During the summer on Friday nights, we have an outdoor movie on a large screen for families to enjoy, in the park across from the library. Everyone brings their own chairs to enjoy the entertainment. A group of teenagers hand out free popcorn for tips."

"That sounds fun! My daughter, Kyra, would like that. Did we miss it?"

"Nope. We've got one more, on Labor Day next weekend; that's the official closing of the season."

"That would be great for Kyra to meet people her own age." Riley shifted her bag with the wicker basket to her other hand. "It was nice to meet you. Hope to see you next weekend then."

"One more thing before you go," Sally said. "If the market on Fifth doesn't have something you want, we might be able to get it." She leaned closer and whispered, "Don't ask my husband Bernie about anything if you're in a hurry. If you do, you'll be here all day. Loves to talk, that man. But all he talks about is fishing, fishing, and more fishing."

Riley straightened and grinned. "Good to know. I like eating fish for dinner, not catching them. That's *really* hard work!" She'd fished once with her Grandpa at Lake Pleasant and hated it.

She felt a buzzing in the pocket of her uniform vest. With the internet service so unreliable, the chief had given her a two-way radio that must be worn at all times. This device just might be the only way to connect with each other.

"Gotta take this. See you later!" Riley waved to Sally as she headed out the door. "Harper here."

"Chief Barnes. I want you to get over to The Shack. Got a call in about a disturbance. Two women acting wild. Where are you?"

Riley immediately recalled the pair of ladies that had gotten off the ferry looking for trouble. The bottle-blonde with the snake tattoo and her red-haired friend, Chloe. Obviously, they'd started their own party.

"At Murphy's Marina." She pulled her map from her pocket. The Shack was six blocks down Sea Otter Street. "I'm on my way."

"No sirens," Barnes said.

She had a portable siren for the top of her little Fiat that she couldn't imagine using anyway. Riley paused and got her bearings. "Uh, well, my car is at the ferry depot."

"*Excuse* me?"

"Well, I thought I was on a meet and greet mission to familiarize myself with the locals, so I've been walking." Her defenses rose.

It sounded like the chief put something over the radio and possibly, *definitely,* cursed.

"It's all right, Chief. I'm six blocks away—I'll be at the bar in five minutes."

"You better! Call in when you get there and let me know what's happening. Sheezus."

The radio went to static.

Chapter Seven

Riley stood on the corner of Main and Sea Otter Lane to consider her options. Traffic on this beautiful sunny day was thick with both vehicles and pedestrians, and going to the ferry depot to get her car was not a smart move.

In a fast-paced stride, she hurried toward the bar. She had her baton and taser, as well as her gun. In the fifteen years since she'd first entered the police force, the only times she'd fired her weapon had been in training.

Phoenix had some rough neighborhoods. Sure, she'd drawn her gun, prepared to fire—you had to be if you took it from your holster—but she'd managed to avoid shooting anyone. Her partner that fateful night should *never* have drawn his weapon to kill the suspect who had been under surveillance. The drug dealer hadn't officially been charged with a crime.

Riley's been through department-mandated counseling after the incident and had a solid grasp on her sworn duty to protect and serve. She had zero qualms about entering the bar to settle the disturbance and imagined Lacey and her friend at the center.

The sign above the rust-colored building was blue and the front door had been painted brown with a brass knob. Rock music escaped from underneath the doorway and an open window.

She took stock of the situation but there was nothing out of the ordinary that she could tell from the sidewalk. As far as she knew, the young women were having a party of two. Disorderly conduct didn't require using her gun.

Laughter, cigarette smoke, fried fish. The song changed from rock to country. Riley opened the door with caution.

The light inside was dim, as befitted a bar, and folks were upright, circling the dance floor and whistling.

"Take it off!" a man cheered.

Riley searched behind the bar for Coby, but he wasn't there. Instead, there was a young lady who looked barely old enough to drink herself at the counter, blending drinks.

"Hi. I'm Officer Harper."

The young woman poured out two frosty margaritas and passed them to the men on the corner seats. They picked up the glasses and jostled their way to the circle.

"Hey." The woman wiped her hands on a bar towel.

"Did you call?"

She shook her head. "But I'm glad someone did. Can you get those two outta here? Lars quit this morning to take a job in Bangor, and we're already short-staffed. Coby had to pick up the fish delivery."

Riley nodded as a tank top went flying over the crowd of chanting drinkers.

"Great," the woman said with an eye roll.

"What are they drinking?"

"I think they came in buzzed and started on tequila."

"Did you cut them off?"

"Their money is good. Cash. So, no."

She put her bag with the wicker basket she'd purchased under the counter. "May I leave this here?"

"Sure."

Riley ambled toward the edge of the circle. She cleared her throat and made a path between those cheering the women on.

She reached the dance floor. Lacey and Chloe were both topless and shimmying butt cheek to butt cheek in a grind.

They could be pros at this dancing thing, Riley thought, and Chloe actually had bills in the waistband of her shorts. Lacey had her shorts unbuttoned to reveal she wasn't wearing underwear.

Riley, in her police uniform, was ignored as the dancers held a captive audience. She crossed the floor and unplugged the jukebox. The crowd booed.

"Show's over. Go on home, ladies."

"I'll take you home," one of the guys with a margarita offered.

Lacey pouted. Chloe covered her breasts with her hands, her long purple nails hiding very little. She seemed slightly worried. Or ashamed?

"If you don't go home, I'll have to take you to the station." The department had a whopping three jail cells in the building behind the main office.

Riley raised her radio.

Lacey snorted but realized the party was over.

"What's going on here? Get some damn clothes on! We don't run a strip club, Lacey," Coby said. He'd arrived in the nick of time to see what was happening in his bar.

One enamored and wasted big-bellied gentleman took off his own T-shirt and tossed it to Lacey.

She seductively tugged it over her head.

Riley gestured for Lacey and Chloe to walk before her, out to the sidewalk. "Who are you?" Lacey asked. "You got no right to keep me from having fun. I wasn't doing anythin' wrong!"

Chloe, arm over her breasts, shook her head at her friend.

"Public nudity, public intoxication, disturbing the peace," Riley said in a calm voice.

Coby had followed them out to the sidewalk, bringing their tank tops. He gave both to Chloe since Lacey was wearing a borrowed shirt.

"What are you doing here, Lacey?" Coby growled. "I thought you'd moved to Portland."

"I did," she said, listing into Chloe, who tried to keep her upright. "Moved back. Grams and Grandpa kicked the bucket and left me their place. Gonna sell it and go to, go to Vegas."

Chloe nodded. "I don't feel so good."

Coby took her friend by the shoulder. "Are you staying together?"

"We're best friends," Lacey said.

"The house is down this road three blocks." Coby looked at Riley. "You going to toss their asses in jail?"

Riley considered it. "How about you go home and sleep it off. This will be a warning. And don't let me see you back out again tonight."

Chloe started to cry big crocodile tears. "Oh sank, thank you, Ossifer."

Lacey drew herself up. "We'll go home *right now*. Wanna come with us, Coby? For old times' sake?"

"I would rather get run over by a trolley and dragged to my death than spend any time with you."

Chloe clapped her hand to her mouth in surprise.

Lacey flipped him the bird. "Your loss."

The two women stumbled down the street.

"I'm going to follow at a distance to make sure they actually go home," Riley said. "Wanna walk with me and tell me what you know about her?"

Coby lost his charming smile. "All right. Lacey is a conniving bitch. Anything else?"

Riley maintained a slow pace and Coby matched his steps with hers as they stayed a hundred feet behind the singing off-key pair.

In Phoenix, giving a warning in this instance would suffice. She wondered how Chief Barnes expected her to handle it.

She glanced over at Coby. "How long have you known her?"

"I've only been on the island for four years, and Lacey was a mistake I made the first year she visited her grandparents. She ran up a tab, didn't pay, and wanted sex in exchange. I didn't."

"You know where she works in Portland?"

"Not exactly." He rubbed his chin. "I bet she's a stripper."

Riley had concluded the same. Her respect for Coby went up a tiny notch for not taking what Lacey had offered.

The girls hooked a wide left on Heron Road. "Is this the right way still?"

Coby nodded. "It's too bad about her grandparents."

"Did you know them?"

"Not really. I mean, they came in for fish and chips every once in a while but The Shack's probably not their scene. I didn't realize they'd both passed. It must have been recent."

Riley and Coby continued following the girls until they reached a brightly colored single-story home. Lacey went in first, and Chloe traipsed after her.

"Where's your car?" Coby asked, looking around as if he'd suddenly realized she didn't have it.

"I parked at the depot."

"Oh. Well, you can cut through Heron to Ocean, and you'll be right there. Follow the smell of the harbor."

"Wonderful. Thanks for walking with me, Coby."

He winked, back to flirting. "My pleasure. Thanks for your assistance. I sure hope Lacey sells and gets the hell off our island. I'm not the only one who will be glad to see the last of her. Later!"

Coby jogged in the direction they'd come from and Riley continued on to her car. The Fiat was exactly where she'd left it. The ferry was gone which meant meeting Captain Wyatt another time.

She radioed Chief Barnes. "I'm on my way. It was a minor disturbance, and I escorted the ladies home."

"Come back to the station," he said in a serious voice. "We need to go over expected Sandpiper Bay procedures. I don't know how they did things in Phoenix..."

"Yes, Chief. Be there in five."

***

Riley had the weekend off, so Saturday Riley, Susan, and Kyra took the ferry into Bangor for winter clothes that they'd need sooner rather than later.

When Riley had suggested buying handmade items from Miriam Cramer, Kyra had melted into a puddle of teenaged angst about never fitting in.

They shopped all day, on a budget, but knowing she had her job for the next year allowed Riley to open her wallet just a little wider. She even treated for dinner at P.F. Chang's, something they couldn't get on the island.

Riley bought a pair of winter boots and Susan invested in long underwear. "We'll see who is the coziest," she warned when they both declined.

Between the great sales and clothes that Kyra liked, they had a happy ride home to Sandpiper Bay. Being a Saturday night, there were a lot of "happy" folks on the ferry, and Captain Wyatt and Deke kept everyone amused by singing over the speakers. Deke was a juggler as it turned out and had Kyra in stitches when he grabbed her book and camera, tossing them into the air.

"Give those back!" Kyra laughed.

Deke, in short sleeves, had flexed his biceps and the crowd laughed. He'd returned the items with a bow. "Milady."

Kyra accepted them. "Oh! You hurt your arm."

Riley glanced down at the red abrasions on his forearm, but he laughed it off. "No worries, milady; your juggler is clumsy." He fell at her feet and the folks around them applauded.

When they'd reached home, Riley found the bike basket she'd bought and left at The Shack on the front porch with a note from Coby, thanking her again for handling the Lacey situation.

"This is perfect!" Susan said, taking the basket out to admire. "We should get another one for the other bike."

"Sure," Riley agreed. "Melo's is right by the depot. We can go tomorrow."

"Thanks, Mom," Kyra said before going to bed that night. "It's been a really fun day."

It had been. Now that she had a job, and they had a home, she could relax a little. Best laid plans can change on a dime.

Sunday, Kyra woke up with a cold so their outing was postponed and they spent the whole day together, watching movies and eating soup.

It was still one of the best weekends they'd had in a very long time.

Chapter Eight

Monday morning, Riley arrived at work with a plant for her office and a large framed picture of her, her mom, and her daughter, all smiling, to be mounted on the wall as a reminder to maintain a positive attitude.

Last week's bickering with the chief was not how she wanted to spend the next year. She could control her words and actions and combat the chief's barbs with polite smiles. She would take pride in her work.

Honestly, it was like preparing for battle.

She entered her office and put the philodendron in its six-inch pot on the shelf where she could see it next to the two fold-out chairs. Above the chairs she'd replace the map with her family photo.

Matthew knocked on her door and shuffled into her office with a tired smile. "Morning!"

"Good morning. What are you doing here?" She peered closer at his pale cheeks. "Oh, don't tell me you haven't gone home yet?"

"Not yet." Shadows darkened the skin below his eyes and whiskers scuffed his jaw. He leaned against the doorframe and crossed his arms. "We had a disturbance at the Lobster Pot."

"Oh?" Matthew hadn't been in the station Friday afternoon when she'd come back after the bar incident so he couldn't possibly know about Lacey and her best friend Chloe going topless. For dollar bills. "Is Katie all right?"

"Everyone's fine." He blew out a heavy breath. "The main incident was more *outside* the Lobster Pot."

"In the street?" Sandpiper Bay had a lot of people here for the next-to-last weekend before the end of the season and it was their duty to keep them safe.

Matthew nodded glumly. "Had to give them both tickets for drunk and disorderly."

Her stomach clenched. If this was the same pair, yesterday she'd let them off with a warning. Dang it! Chief Barnes had let her know that he expected for Riley to actually use her ticket book and not just let it weigh down her vest.

His eyes glittered. "Katie called it in around one in the morning. I was at the gas station getting a coffee and shooting the breeze with Nathan."

"What happened?" It occurred to her that Matthew probably knew Lacey from when she'd lived here. "It must be hard, laying down the law to a local."

He waved his hand. "Not this particular person. Everyone was glad to see her move off island, believe me."

Before she could ask specifics, the door chimed and Nancy bustled into the lobby with full arms. "Morning, Riley. Matthew." She placed her purse on the desk. "I heard you had a busy night."

His lip jutted out like Kyra's when she was pouting. "From who?"

"I stopped in at the bakery"—Nancy raised a box of pastries—"and Joan Higgins told me."

Matthew sighed. "Who needs a newspaper with her as the local gossip?"

Riley hid a smile. Between Joan and Coby, she knew who to go to for the latest.

"Well, what happened?" Nancy stepped toward Matthew, and Riley got up from her office chair. "I heard that Katie had to kick Lacey and a girlfriend out of the restaurant for lewd behavior. Some of the other diners jumped in to help."

That sounded about right to Riley, who'd witnessed it for herself at The Shack.

Matthew eyed the ceiling. "Not quite that big of a scene. Katie asked them to leave, and they eventually did."

Nancy grinned. "Come on, Matthew. Give us the details. I heard they were drunk as skunks and dancing in the street."

"Yeah, guess they were. But they quieted down after I handed them citations and went on home. I followed them to make sure. Lacey and..."

Riley recalled the snake tattoo on Lacey's neck and the unabashed nakedness of the girls at Coby's bar. "Her friend was Chloe."

Matthew's jaw dropped and he snapped it closed. "How'd you know that?"

"I had a run-in with them yesterday in the middle of the day. They'd been drinking and disrupted the peace at The Shack."

"Did you cite them? I didn't see anything in the computer log."

She shook her head. "Let them off with a warning. I'm sorry."

"Well, how could you know?" Matthew shrugged. "You were probably being nice, since you're new and all."

"Chief reamed me, so I won't make that mistake again. If there's a call that deserves to be ticketed, I need to not be *lazy*, as I must have been in Phoenix." She perched on the edge of her desk.

"Sorry about that. Chief Barnes..."

"You don't have to explain, Matthew. It's all right. I've got a tough hide."

Nancy joined Matthew and offered him the pastry box. "Her poor grandparents must be rolling in their graves. Such nice, down-to-earth folks. They spoiled her, since she was their only family left."

"Spoiled rotten." Matthew opened the box and breathed in the sugary scent of donuts. He selected an apple fritter. "I've done my report and I'm about to head home for some sleep. This will hit the spot, Nance."

"Enjoy!" Nancy hustled down the hall with the Bake and Shake box and started to make coffee in the kitchen.

Riley and Matthew compared a few notes on the intoxicated Lacey and Chloe.

"I wonder how long she's in town?" Matthew bit into the fritter.

"I think she came in on the ferry Friday morning. I was at the vendors along the harbor and she was flirting pretty hard with some of the guys that had gotten off. She invited them to her place to party, but they were more interested in camping at Mackabee's. They heard that the woods are haunted."

Matthew paused mid-bite. "Rumors. Some of the fishermen perpetuate the stories, saying it's good for tourism."

Riley wondered about that but didn't press. "She wants to sell the cottage she inherited from her grandparents and move to Vegas."

"Vegas? It's a shame Lacey turned out the way she did—but she was always a bad apple," Matthew said with uncharacteristic harshness. "My mom likes everyone, but she detests Lacey Killian."

Seemed a lot of people did not care for Lacey.

"See you later, Riley." Matthew went out, and after a few minutes the chief came in.

"Morning, Chief," Riley called cordially, determined to put her best foot forward.

He blinked in surprise. "Morning?"

The reception phone rang, and Nancy rounded the desk to sit down and answer it. "Sandpiper Bay Police Department," she said cheerily.

Her face paled after a moment of listening. "Darren?"

She nodded, her blond hair sliding forward.

Riley watched, sensing a change in the air. The chief waited too.

"Oh, no. I'll send someone over right now." Nancy hung up and looked at them with wide blue eyes. "That was Darren Williams, over at the lighthouse."

"Yeah?" Chief Barnes gestured for her to continue.

"He says there's a body on the rocks." Nancy gulped.

Riley and the chief exchanged a look. How did he want to handle this? Friday he'd lit into her for not following procedure. She would follow his lead.

At last he said, "Ride with me, Harper. We'll go check it out. Probably a drowning."

A drowning. That made sad sense when you considered they were surrounded by the sea.

In Phoenix there would be numbers to call, like the medical examiner and possibly an ambulance. "I never asked, but do we have an ambulance on the island?"

"First responders from the fire station. Let's scout the scene first," the chief said. "It might be nothing."

Riley kept her opinion on that to herself. In her mind, there should be more players in the team involved. Protocol here might vary from the city.

She eyed the SUV before climbing into the passenger side. There was a silver box in the very rear. Her Fiat didn't have that, just the basic first aid stuff. Flares, a blanket, a tire iron. Attachable siren.

"I've got an investigation kit in the back," he explained with a scowl. She hoped it wasn't toward her as he drove away from the station. "You get to know folks on the island. My first year here we had a bad storm and a fishing boat sank. Lost two local men and it really rocked the community."

"The storms are that bad? The worse I've been in is a monsoon."

"They can be." He drummed his thumb to the steering wheel. "In this case the men were caught by surprise. The ocean deserves respect. Never get too comfortable."

"You don't have to tell me twice," she assured him. "I made sure that Kyra had swimming lessons from the time she was three."

He chuckled wryly. "No ocean in Arizona."

"No. But we had a pool, and we'd vacation at Lake Pleasant. This is still a big change."

Chief turned and followed a narrow road that led to the lighthouse. "Here we are." He parked at the white base. The top half was painted red. A tall, thin man in khakis paced like a caged lion before a yellow door.

"Who is that?"

"Darren Williams." He took the keys from the ignition. "He rents the rooms at the bottom here."

"Is he a caretaker?"

"Sort of. He's good man." Barnes gave her a steady glare as if daring her to argue. "Did his time overseas."

The chief slipped out of the SUV without saying more. Wind buffeted Riley as she followed. She'd only been here a week and the weather had already changed.

"Darren, this is Officer Riley Harper." Barnes kept his tone low and friendly. "New to Sandpiper Bay."

"Hey, Darren, it's nice to meet you." Riley noticed his hands were in his pockets so she kept the introduction short. She scanned the grass and rocks around them for anything out of place. Where was the body? The ocean was beyond the cliff face the lighthouse was on. "How's it going?"

The man shuffled his feet. The guy could be in his twenties or nearing forty. It was hard to tell as the lines in his face were probably due to his military service rather than actual age. He wore muddy brown boots, hunched his shoulders, and had a wildness in his brown eyes that matched his frenetic energy.

When he spoke his voice was rough and gravelly. "Could be better. Could be better. Could be a lot better."

"Can you show us, Darren?" Riley didn't know the chief was capable of being so calm and cool.

Darren's jaw clenched and he rocked on his feet. "Not good, Chief." He jerked his head to the ocean. "Down there."

He scrambled nimbly down a narrow sandy path that he probably used every day. No foliage grew among the rocks and boulders.

"Male or female?" Riley asked the veteran, staying on his heels.

Darren didn't answer but raced ahead.

The chief was third in the party, a little less nimble due to his girth. Riley slid on some loose rocks but righted herself. *Slow and steady or you'll fall on your butt. Barnes already thinks you're a hazard.*

At last she and Barnes reached the beach below the lighthouse.

Darren, agitated, strode toward an outcropping of rocks, partially submerged in the water. He pointed and then looked away.

Riley squinted into the waves and gasped. She was not new to death, but it never got easy.

The supine body, female, was naked, her face battered beyond recognition. Bottle-blond hair swirled in the ocean, a pale hand drifted toward the shore as if the dead woman pleaded for help though she was beyond saving. Bruises had formed along her crushed side and hip.

Chief cursed, then pointed to the top of the lighthouse where Darren lived. "Probably a jumper. It wouldn't be the first suicide here. It's a popular spot, unfortunately."

Riley wasn't so quick to conclude anything at the moment. Other variables might come into play. She wished she had some binoculars to check out the gallery around the top of the lighthouse. She'd have to go see it. The incline was a good hundred feet.

"Lovers make suicide pacts." Barnes rubbed his jaw and pain flashed in his eyes. "Winters can be long here."

Darren trembled and shivered, stomping his boots to the packed sand. "It's not for everyone."

"When did you find the body?" Riley asked Darren.

He patted his chest and stuck his hands in his pockets. She noticed that he had damp patches on his pants, as if he'd kneeled in the sand or fallen.

"Darren?" Chief Barnes spoke gently. "When did you find her?"

"What? A half hour or so. I called as soon as I saw her."

"Do you know who it is?" Chief asked Darren.

Darren's jaw clenched hard.

Riley scanned the sandy area. The rocks and the body were three feet in the sea. "Is this high tide? Would the body have been in the sand and not the water?"

"We can check the tide times in the paper or on the website." Chief Barnes's shoulders turned rigid.

She feared she might step on her boss's toes, but she didn't think he was questioning Darren hard enough. The man definitely knew more than what he was saying.

"Jumping from the deck and landing on the sand would have a different impact on the body than if she landed on the rocks," Chief remarked.

Riley scanned the beach of rock and driftwood that was getting skinnier by the minute as the water encroached. "Let's hope any evidence hasn't been washed away."

"The beach disappears at high tide. We should hurry," Darren said. A tic formed below his left eye.

She glanced at the poor broken body of the young woman as a wave shifted it. Her blond locks floated away from her neck. Tattoos covered her arms. Most telling was the tip of the snake around the girl's throat.

"I know her." Riley put a hand to her mouth. "That's Lacey Killian. Matthew gave her a ticket last night. I'd only given her a warning on Friday."

"She's a bad girl," Darren muttered.

Barnes stared from the body on the rocks, to Darren, to Riley. He seemed immobile.

She stepped toward the waves, soaking her boots. "Shouldn't we try to bring her body to shore? We're losing evidence by the second."

The chief clamped his lips together and pointed directly above them to the gallery deck around the top of the lighthouse. "No evidence needed. This is a clear suicide."

Riley acknowledged to herself that a leap from the lighthouse to the rocks below would explain the battered condition of the dead woman's body. It's just that she'd been trained to not accept the obvious.

"We should call for a medical examiner before we tamper with the body," she replied.

Barnes pulled his phone from his pocket. "Damn it. No cell service down in this cove. You, Harper?"

Riley pulled out her phone. Not a single bar. She shook her head and turned to Darren to catch him off guard. "Where are Lacey's clothes?"

Darren pointed a shaking finger toward a large boulder behind them on the beach. "There."

Had he put the clothes there? Had he and Lacey been involved? It was obvious the man was distraught. Guilty behavior? The chief was acting strangely too.

Riley was in a race against the incoming tide, so she braced herself for the cold Atlantic and strode into the surf. Three feet out, the water hit her knees and she was at Lacey's side.

She examined the body as best she could. The water would have washed away any DNA but there might be a clue to find. Lacey's arm was wedged between two rocks so the body wasn't going anywhere.

Lacey had been drinking heavily last night. Had she killed herself? Riley knew the young woman had wanted to sell her grandparents' cottage and move to Vegas. Those plans didn't equal suicidal thoughts. Riley's teeth chattered as she studied the clotted mass of hair around the skull. Was that a hit? Or had Lacey managed to strike a rock just so when she jumped?

If Lacey *had* jumped. Riley supposed it was possible that she'd gotten some crazy idea to climb the long circular staircase. Maybe show off for somebody? Where was Chloe? She turned to Darren. "Did you see Lacey on the lighthouse? Did you hear anything?"

He glanced at her, then away. She shivered and blamed it on the cold. Not for the look in his eyes.

Riley took note of the lacerations on the side of Lacey's face, though the water prevented any blood. Her hair had been knotted with seaweed.

"Get out of the water, Officer Harper," Barnes said. "You'll get a chill. I don't have time for you to get pneumonia."

Riley noticed the hands...no rings. A broken red fingernail. And most importantly, she noticed bruising around the woman's wrists.

"Chief Barnes. I don't think this is a suicide. These bruises indicate she was held forcibly."

"Don't touch anything." The chief stayed at the edge of the water.

Darren hugged his arms tight around his shaking body. "What are you saying?"

Riley looked right at Darren. Twitchy Darren, Darren who'd called in the dead body. Who knew where Lacey's clothes were. Would he break if she pressed him? "I don't think this was an accident."

Chapter Nine

Riley was not the kind of police officer to shirk her duty or look the other way. Hence the reason she was in Sandpiper Bay in the first place.

She slogged herself out of the water with wet boots and cold pants, her body's core frigid. Just because the chief had this protective vibe for Darren didn't mean she had to play along. Proof would lead her to whoever had harmed Lacey.

Barnes waited for the clouds to clear and tried his cell phone again. "Yes!"

He called in the medical examiner and the paramedics to load the body and bring Lacey to the small two-story hospital and morgue. The chief had an attitude, but he stepped back while Riley questioned Darren more thoroughly.

"Did you see Lacey last night? Or hear voices?"

Darren's eyes darted from Lacey, to her clothes, then to Riley. He thrummed his fingers against his thigh. *Ratatat.*

No answer.

"Please, Darren. You called us, which was the proper thing to do. All we want is the truth." She needed to calm him down so she could get some straight answers.

He gave her the stink eye. "I didn't do it."

Uh-huh. She'd heard more claims of innocence in her time on the force than she'd heard confessions. "We aren't saying that at all. If you could tell me when you saw her, and the circumstances, that will help us find out what happened."

"She's a mean woman. Bad."

Riley understood that Lacey had few friends on the island. Would that make finding out what happened to her more difficult? Or easier?

"Was she *bad* to you?"

"Yes. Cursed me out when I asked her to go home."

The warmth of adrenaline rushed through her. She stayed outwardly calm. "Last night?"

He hesitated, then nodded and pulled his hands from his pockets.

Riley dropped her gaze to his hands. The knuckles were red and abraded.

Should she be on guard around this man? She glanced at the chief, but he was waving to the paramedics at the top of the hill.

Two men carefully brought a stretcher down.

Darren's fingers shook. She knew he might shut down fast, but she needed a little more from him first.

"Were you together?" Riley smiled, nonjudgmental. "Like, on a date?"

"No!" His voice broke and he said again, "No. Nothing like that. I saw her. Climbing the stairs. My lighthouse. No one's allowed up there after seven. I told her that. She cursed at me."

"I see." Had they fought? Had he manhandled her and accidentally let her slip? Or did he throw her over to the rocks? "Was she naked when you saw her?"

His cheeks turned crimson. "Yes."

Chief Barnes was suddenly at her side. "Gah. Darren, were you sleeping with Lacey?"

"No. No, sir. I don't like her."

Did he not like Lacey enough to kill her?

"Headache. I need to go lie down." Darren eyed the lighthouse at the top of the hill as if it were his sanctuary.

"We have more questions," Riley started to say.

"I'll be by later," the chief said, overriding her. "Go on now."

She bit back a retort and stepped out of the way as Darren raced up the embankment.

Chief Barnes snapped photos with his cell phone as Lacey was brought from the water by the paramedics. "Why don't you run up and get an evidence bag from the back of my SUV? It's in the silver box."

Riley nodded. Being the secondary officer in this case, she didn't take offense. Besides, she was in much better shape to scurry up and down the hill without causing a heart attack. As she reached the top, she looked at the yellow door.

Darren was already inside.

What was up with the chief, anyway, insisting it would be a suicide without looking at all the facts? It was not how things were done. Maybe he wanted to retire with a spotless record? That would make no sense in the city, but here was a different world.

Riley brought the kit down and walked around the boulder where the clothes were. She put on gloves before depositing a red sequined dress into the plastic evidence bag. Red lacy underwear and bra, neatly folded. Lacey must have taken the clothes off, or else whoever she'd been with last night was a neat freak. Chloe had been just as sloppy in her tank top and short shorts.

Riley should not have contradicted her boss when he called the death a suicide, but the truth was, Lacey's death seemed suspicious. Her job as an officer of the Sandpiper Bay Police Department was to find out what had happened to the dead woman that nobody liked.

The truth, not conjecture.

She looked around the boulder, but it was all sand and there were no footprints, not even Darren's around the rock, though his boot prints were along the water's edge.

Peering upward, she saw the white belly of the lighthouse. The bottom of the circular metal walkway. The railing around the gallery deck was four feet high.

Easy enough to climb over or get pushed over.

She walked along the other side of the beach below the lighthouse. There was a metal stairway curving around the building to the gallery above. This would be the only way up unless Darren opened the door and invited her in.

"I'm going up," she said to Barnes.

"Suit yourself." He stayed by the stretcher.

Riley brought the kit with her and climbed the rocky path on the left side, while the chief followed the paramedics up the right.

She searched around the base of the lighthouse, aware of Darren on the inside. Had he pushed Lacey off in a rage, or had they hooked up and things went sour? Where was Lacey's friend, Chloe?

Riley wanted a picture of the scrapes on Darren's knuckles.

She climbed the outside staircase, noticing the metal was bolted to the cement. It was sturdy, but she didn't care for heights.

It had been a lesson early on to not show weakness, so she gritted her teeth and continued climbing until she reached the narrow walkway on top. She walked to the edge and looked over the rail at the deadly rocks and waves below.

What was that on the gallery deck?

She knelt down and picked up a red fingernail.

Darren had been telling the truth about Lacey being up here. She put the fingernail in the plastic bag, then examined the red cement top around the light. She'd learned online that it was behind mesh to withstand the storms on Maine's coast.

Paint was buckled by the extreme weather.

Was that blood on the wall? Say, from knuckles scraping it? She took a picture and put a sample of the paint into another evidence bag. There were only five in the kit, so she'd have to restock it soon.

In Phoenix they'd have a forensics team to do this kind of work, but here, she was it.

She descended the metal staircase where the chief was on the phone, speaking curtly. He saw her and gestured to the SUV, ending the call.

"I almost left you here. What were you doing?"

She opened the back and piled in the evidence bags. "Looking for clues. We should come with a better camera and a DNA kit."

"What are you talking about?" He faced her, his arms crossed. She shut the back of the SUV.

"Lacey was up there, all right. I found a broken fingernail."

"Jumped." He shook his head stubbornly. "No way did Darren do it. I knew his daddy. We served together but he never made it home. He's got his demons but he's no killer."

"Chief, those bruises around her wrists lead me to believe that there was a struggle. With who, we don't know."

"You arrived here wanting to prove yourself so you're making more of this than you need to."

She exhaled and kept calm. "I also saw the abrasions on Darren's knuckles. They might match a swash of blood on the wall up there. I took a sample."

His eyes narrowed.

"We need a picture of Darren's hands and a blood sample."

"You need to leave that man alone."

"He was nervous, Chief. Why is that? Unless he has something to hide. Why was Lacey naked?"

"He said he wasn't sleeping with her."

"People, especially guilty people, lie."

"He has PTSD. The man's a hero for what he saw overseas. I won't have you bothering him with unnecessary questions. He's a trained killer—of the enemy. Not floozies."

She lifted her chin, not backing down. "Let's see if the blood samples match."

"You're a real pain, Harper."

"Just doing my job, Chief."

She didn't blink or look away as he glared at her.

"Fine," he said at last. "We've got the medical examiner coming over from the mainland. Martin should be here by three. Until then Lacey will be on ice at the hospital."

"Should we go another round with Darren while we're here, then?"

"Let the man rest. He's not going anywhere. We can call Matthew in to assist." They got in the car and he started the engine. "You found a fingernail?"

"Red." She buckled up. "I noticed that Lacey was missing one."

"Why did you get in the water? Were you trying to make me look bad?"

"This isn't personal. I was trained to do things a certain way. Maybe different than you. Why are you so certain that it's suicide?"

"It's a popular jump spot. We had two others in my time and my predecessor told me about the doomed lovebirds."

"So Lacey would have known about it too." She nodded to concede that he had a point.

"Yep."

Then she brought up one of her own. "If Lacey was going to kill herself, why would she neatly fold her clothes?"

He tapped the wheel as he drove toward the station. "Dang it if I know. Guess we better start asking questions. You can start as soon as we get back, since you're so sure that something else happened."

"I'm not sure of anything, except that Lacey is dead."

"I'll send Sniders over to talk to Darren. You can talk to her neighbors."

If he thought he was punishing her, he was wrong. She wanted to track down Chloe. Question Katie about what had happened last night outside her restaurant.

"Fine with me."

"When the coroner comes back with probable suicide, we will see who's right."

"Yes." Riley would bet her next month's salary that Lacey hadn't committed suicide.

No, but what if, because she'd been drunk, she'd accidentally drowned?

She loved investigating and uncovering clues—her love of true crime mysteries had led her into her career in the police force.

Accidents happened all the time.

Murder happened more often than people realized.

They reached the station and brought the evidence bags to the back room to be logged and photographed later.

"Well?" Nancy asked. "What happened?"

Riley looked at the chief.

"We discovered the body of Lacey Killian in the water below the lighthouse."

"Oh no!" Nancy brought her fingers to her mouth. "Did she jump?"

The chief raised his brow at Riley as if to say, see?

"We don't know for sure," the chief said. "Officer Harper will be conducting the investigation."

"Ohhh," Nancy crooned, wide-eyed.

"I'll be in my office," he said. "I'm expecting a call from the medical examiner so patch him through."

"I will." Nancy nodded with her whole body.

The chief glanced at Riley. "Make sure to document everything before you leave to talk to the neighbors. We want to follow the law to the letter."

Riley's cheeks heated. He went into his office and slammed the door.

Nancy busied herself with the computer.

She'd had such high hopes for having a positive week. Now she was being tested to solve the mystery of this woman's death.

Riley examined the clear bags of possible evidence. What did she really have to work with? Fingernail. Clothes. Paint chip.

It took an hour to get things into the computer, and by then she had some questions ready. The only way to unravel a mystery was to uncover one clue at a time. She'd start with Lacey's broken fingernail and her friend, Chloe.

Chapter Ten

Riley studied the evidence spread out on the long rectangular table in the rear of the department behind Nancy's desk. She'd triple-checked to make sure she hadn't missed anything.

"Hey, Nancy?"

"Yes?"

"Will you make sure that nobody touches this stuff until I get back? I've logged it all in, but I'm antsy to go talk to Chloe, Lacey's friend." She'd been dragging her feet to see if the coroner would call, but it was almost one and breakfast had worn off long ago.

Nancy's eyes were bright as she gave Riley an admiring smile. "Sure! That was really something," she spoke softly and glanced at the chief's closed office door. "You've practically won him over."

"Well, I wouldn't say that, exactly." Riley made sure she had her ticket book and a pen in her vest. Notebook. Charged radio. "We plan to keep things professional around here and start working together. Put our egos aside and do our jobs."

"Thank heavens!" Nancy snickered. "Things were getting kind of ugly."

"True. Now, as long as I don't botch this case up, our working relationship should improve." She gave a wry smile. "I'm going to do my best to make sure that doesn't happen."

Chief Barnes stepped out of his office and glared at Riley. "What are you still doing here? That Chloe girl will have time to catch the ferry and hightail it to China before you can let her know that her friend is dead."

"Just leaving," Riley said. *What a grump.* "Will you call me when you get the coroner report?"

"Yep. He's a very competent man so you take your time and find out as much as you can about why Lacey was here, who she was with...well. You know the drill."

She did indeed. Nodding to Nancy, Riley pushed open the door. "Wish me luck!"

Barnes didn't answer but Nancy crossed her fingers. Riley's steps were lighter than they'd been for a week as she headed for her car. If one could really call it that. Looked more like a large blue snail.

Riley drove straight to Lacey's house and knocked on the front door. No answer. Someone had kept up the lawn with a recent mow. Yellow geraniums were in cobalt-blue pots by the door. She knocked again. Nothing.

Second stop was Bake and Shake bakery to gather both information and satisfy her rumbling stomach. The outdoor seating area had no tables free and inside was three-quarters full.

There wouldn't be much time for conversation, but she went to the counter and caught Joan's eye, smiling brightly.

"Good to see you again, Officer!" Joan patted down her apron for a pen. "What can I get for you?"

"A slice of your quiche and a bottled water to go. I'd hoped to ask a couple of questions, but I see that you're busy."

"Not too busy for you," Joan replied. She gestured to the packed interior. "Everyone already has their orders so that should keep them happy. Come on back to the counter seat and we can chat for a few minutes."

"Thank you."

Joan rushed off to get Riley's order.

Riley sat down on the stool, fiddling with the salt and pepper shakers as she watched Joan bop from one spot to the next, sharing a smile or quick word with everyone. Joan was a hub for gossip and must have heard that a body had been discovered that morning. Few people knew the body was that of Lacey Killian.

Joan brought over the quiche and a bottle of water. "Sorry about that," she said, leaning forward. "Is this regarding what happened at the lighthouse?"

"It is. I'm going to ask you to keep what we talk about under wraps until I give you the go ahead, all right?"

Joan made the motion of buttoning her lips.

Riley nodded, trusting Joan. "You must know almost everyone who's lived in Sandpiper Bay. Do you remember a young girl named Lacey who lived with her grandparents? She moved away a few years ago."

"That would be Lacey Killian. Of course I remember her. She was a terror! Broke her grandparents' hearts when she took off like that. She'd come back to the island when she'd get into trouble or needed some cash."

"That would be the one. When was the last time you saw her?"

"She didn't come into the bakery, but she was with a little red-haired lass, dancing in the street, Friday night it was."

So the two hadn't stayed home like they'd said they would. "Just them?"

Joan tapped her finger to her chin. "I told Charlie at the time that those girls were being followed. He told me that they were acting, they were encouraging male company. I let it go, because the truth is, Lacey was a bit loose. I did think it was strange."

"What did the person following them look like?"

"Oh, it was too dark to really tell. A man for sure. He had a baseball cap on. Taller than Lacey. At least six feet."

She thought of the guys who'd camped in Mackabee's Park. Were they still there? She had to find Chloe.

"Have you seen the red-haired young woman?"

"No. Sorry."

Just then four customers came in.

"Thank you for your time, Joan. Appreciate the information and the quiche." She ate another quick bite, then put a twenty on the table.

Joan put her hand over Riley's and asked quietly, "Is Lacey the girl at the lighthouse?"

"We don't have a positive identification."

"Hmm. Poor soul. Lots of people have jumped from that lighthouse."

Riley kept her expression neutral, but Joan's brow quirked. "You think it wasn't an accident?"

"Joan, I'm just gathering information right now. Please don't arrive at false conclusions or discuss this, all right?" While Riley was perfectly fine listening to others blab, but she needed to be closemouthed. "Thanks for the tip. I'll bring my mom and daughter here this weekend."

Joan gave a regal nod. "You be sure to do that."

Riley got into the Fiat and started the engine. She tapped the steering wheel. Should she track down the guys in the woods? Or try Chloe at Lacey's again first?

If she were Chloe, she might not want to talk to the police, especially if she already knew her friend was dead.

Five minutes later Riley was parked in the drive. She walked around the entire house first, wondering why anyone would want to sell this piece of property. The location was ideal. Close to the main street but secluded, with only two other cottages in sight.

A perfect rental income stream if Lacey didn't want to live here full time.

She took the red-painted steps and was about to knock on the door when it opened. Chloe stood there in tight yoga pants and a halter top, with a cigarette dangling from her mouth and a scowl on her face. Her bare feet were dirty.

"What are *you* doing here?" she asked, blowing the smoke in her direction. Obviously any warm feelings Chloe had for Riley after giving her a free ride at The Shack had disappeared.

"Is Lacey here?"

Chloe's toe tapped the top step. "No."

"Where is she?"

"Out. She likes to go for runs. Keeps in shape."

Riley would have pegged Lacey's extreme thinness on partying, not exercise, but she didn't call Chloe's bluff.

"Heard you two were partying pretty hard last night at the Lobster Pot. What happened?"

"Nothing. Had dinner, a little too much to drink, and by that time she was stumbling all over the place, so figured I should get her back home." Chloe put a hand on her bony hip and gave Riley a hard stare. "No crime in that."

"No, ma'am." Riley balanced her weight on the bottom step in case Chloe made a run for it. "Except that it wasn't all that happened, was it? My fellow officer, Officer Sniders, had to give you both tickets for disturbing the peace."

Chloe winced and took another deep drag of her smoke. "Things got out of hand, I'll admit."

As "things" tended to do when alcohol and drugs were involved. "When was the last time you saw Lacey?"

"Not sure. I was pretty whacked after leaving the restaurant. Came home and went to bed right away. I heard Lacey leave, talking about the full moon on the beach. I figured she went swimming in the nude to touch base with her spiritual side. Maybe she's passed out somewhere?"

"Have you been here all morning?"

"Yeah." She glanced toward the secluded beach, hugging her arm to her waist, smoke from her cigarette trailing upward. "I was getting worried, then I saw you outside." Chloe peeked at Riley. "Has something happened?"

"I'm sorry to inform you, but Lacey Killian is dead."

"No!" She fell back with slack fingers; her cigarette hit the lawn by the steps and her face went white. "How? Did you catch the guy who did it?"

Riley tilted her head to study the sincerity of Chloe's reactions. "I didn't say she was murdered or hurt by a man. It might have been a suicide."

"No way," Chloe insisted. "That girl loved life—Lacey was a real party whore. And after the sale of this property? She'd be set up for life." She pinched off the burning ember of the cigarette and tossed the dead butt to the grass.

Riley walked to the top stair and gestured to the open door. "Do you mind if I come in for a few minutes? You're her best friend and might know more than you think you do. We've got to find out what happened...if you're sure she wouldn't commit suicide?" This made it seem like Riley needed Chloe's help, and Chloe slowly nodded.

"Yeah. But don't overstay your welcome, 'kay?" Chloe waved Riley in after her, into a six-foot-long hall. At the end of the corridor was a spacious living room overlooking the bay. The furniture was a little dated, but the enormous brick fireplace made up for that.

How could Lacey want to leave all this? And yet the question didn't deserve an answer. Lacey wanted the high life and being stuck on a remote island would be worse than death.

"Mind if I sit?" She stepped toward an oval oak table with three oak chairs.

"Nope. Go ahead."

Riley followed Chloe into and eighties-style gray-and-peach-colored kitchen with old wooden cabinets and laminate counters. There was a narrow window above the sink. The house needed a little remodeling, but it was adorable.

Riley took a seat on an oak chair in the kitchen nook and Chloe joined her. Instead of meeting her eye, she picked at her purple nails that were chipped and cracked. She remembered that Chloe'd had a fresh manicure at The Shack. What had Chloe been up to in the past two days? She scratched her arm.

"When was the last time you saw her?"

"Like I said. I went to bed after we got our tickets from Officer Cutie. Boy, she tried to get him to not give us those tickets. Even offered a BJ but he turned her down. Not many guys would do that."

Poor Matthew, Riley thought. He hadn't mentioned that part earlier at the station. Had he been protecting Lacey for some reason? Nah, that didn't make sense.

"Like I said, I heard Lacey leave," Chloe was saying, "and she wasn't here in the morning."

Riley gestured to Chloe's toes. "Looks like you were digging up worms or something. Maybe you partied too hard and don't remember what happened when you got home."

Chloe wiggled her toes and scratched at the hem of her tight yoga pants. "I remember. It's the way I told it."

Riley didn't argue. She needed to tread carefully. "You must have felt awful when she wasn't here this morning. Did you think to call the police?"

"I was worried." Her expression turned cunning as she eyed Riley. "But it wasn't my fault."

Riley nodded and folded her hands on the table. She didn't want Chloe to get nervous and clam up. "Of course it wasn't. She's the one who was up in that lighthouse in the middle of the night."

Instead of coming home, had they walked the beach and climbed up the lighthouse together? Perhaps they argued, or maybe she stumbled? Not murder but an accident caused by too much alcohol and bad judgment.

But what about Darren? He said he'd seen her and yelled at her to get away. Had he seen two women, or just one who was drunk and wouldn't leave?

"What lighthouse?" Chloe demanded, pounding the table. "Not that one with the creepy military guy living at the bottom floor? Lacey knew him from before." She snickered. "She knew all the boys, if you know what I mean."

Riley cleared her throat as her stomach knotted. Back to Darren again. "Did you ladies talk to him?"

Chloe shrugged coyly.

"Remember, Chloe, that you are not in any trouble. We're investigating Lacey's death and just need to dig a little deeper into her life."

"Okay. But I don't know much. Only met her four years ago."

Riley took out her notebook and pen. "Lacey didn't like this island, or the people, and wanted to sell her inheritance and run to Vegas."

"To be a showgirl. I was going to go too."

"Is that right? Hmm. She lived with her grandparents and not her parents. Why was that? Did she have a troubled childhood? Was she a wild child way back then? Did she push her parents away, or did they push her?" Riley was offering suggestions to see if Chloe reacted to any of them.

Zilch. Chloe's hazel eyes were streaked with red and she scratched absently at her ankle. "She never said much about her early days and I never asked. We met in Bangor and both worked at the same club. We started hanging together and had a good time. That's about it."

"I'm sure you did. The questions I'm going to ask are no reflection on you or your lifestyle so you can be completely open." Riley touched her hand, still looking at those chipped nails. Climbing after Lacey? Her story of going home to bed didn't make sense. Chloe was as much a party girl as Lacey. "She said she lived in Portland?"

"Yeah. We both got a promotion to headline at an elite club so I went with her."

"Just like you were going to go with her to Vegas."

"That's right." Chloe stood up to take a bottle of water out of the fridge. "Want one?"

"No, thanks." Riley waited until Chloe was seated again. She'd bet the girl had gotten up because she was nervous. Was she scratching out of nerves too? Why would she be nervous unless she was lying? "Who else did you all hang out with the past few days? Did you ever meet up with the guys who'd been camping?"

She thought back. "No. Too bad. They were adorbs."

"So, you were having fun on the island. What happened last night?"

Chloe exhaled and added an eye roll. "Lacey likes being the center of attention, you know? Last night was no different. Too bad for us, that witch Katie and Lacey got into it, something to do with when Lacey lived here as a kid. It pissed Lacey off that Katie had a boyfriend and they owned the restaurant."

"How strange..."

"I didn't catch it all, but I got the impression Lacey had a secret that scared Katie." Chloe looked around the kitchen nervously as she rubbed her heavily tattooed arms. The girl was as toned as a gym trainer. *Or stripper.* Strong enough to push a woman to her death?

"How long after this altercation did you both leave? Were you alone?"

Chloe frowned and reached for the package of cigarettes on the counter. "Why do you keep asking me that? We might have picked up stragglers—that's usually how we roll. Can't be the life of the party without a party. Anyway, I dropped a hundred for the bill, grabbed her by the arm, and dragged her outside." She smacked a smoke from the pack. "Her black mood disappeared like that."

"And she was still okay when Officer Sniders arrived?"

"Not *okay,* okay. She hates this island and everybody on it. I understand why she wanted to start over. Everybody here sees her, saw her, as the bad seed."

Riley jotted that down. Her suspect list kept growing. "Was she addicted to drugs? Uppers, X, heroin?"

"No." Chloe shook her head. "Recreation only. Justin wouldn't allow a druggie in his club."

Riley's pulse raced. "Justin? Who is that?"

"He owns the club in Portland that we both worked at. Exotic dancers." She tapped the unlit cigarette on the table. "I am not ashamed of that and neither was Lacey."

"You shouldn't be. This might be a good starting point though. Was there anyone in the club, a patron for example that she might have offended, or someone who came in often to watch her dance? A person obsessed with her. If he couldn't have her than no one will. That kind of thing?" Riley thought of what Joan had told her, about someone following the young women Friday night.

"Not that I know of." Chloe flicked the lighter but didn't light up. "She was having an affair with Justin, the owner, but broke it off when she heard about her grandparents' deaths and that she was the heir."

"How did that go over, with him losing his two lead dancers?"

She blushed. "He was angry—probably thought we made him look like a fool. Justin was very controlling, to her, to the dancers."

"Why did you stay so long?"

"He always made us feel safe. We didn't have to do anything on the side, you know?" She took a slug of her water. "Justin was crazy about her."

Riley held Chloe's gaze. "So, think of it like this. What if he felt that Lacey had stripped him of his pride, blowing him aside as soon as she had money of her own. That could make a man crazy enough to follow her here and take care of his own business."

Chloe tossed her head back and forth. "No, no, no. Guy's not perfect, that's for sure. But he'd never hurt her, I'm positive." She jutted her chin. "He protects his 'girls' and that's why we stay with him. Not for the lousy money."

Should she mention the man seen following them the other night? Chloe might need to protect herself. Unless she was lying. Riley tapped her pen to the notepad. "I will need his full name and the club's address."

Chloe bit her bottom lip. "No. I don't want to squeal on him. He's innocent, I know. He wouldn't kill Lacey."

"If that's true, then it will be no problem to question him and cross him off the list."

"What list?" Chloe squeaked. "A *suspect* list? No way." She lifted her chin in defiance. "Am I on it too?" The lighter flicked and flicked but never caught.

"You've been straight with me," Riley stretched the truth on that one, "and obviously you care about your friend, and your boss, Justin. You are a loyal person."

"I am." Chloe looked at her lap and a few tears slid down her cheek.

Guilt, perhaps? "Tell me more about Justin?" When Chloe remained silent, Riley prodded her again. "We'll find out the information regardless. Just might take us a little longer. A Google search will do it."

At that her shoulders slumped. "Justin DiCaprio. The Kitty Cat Club isn't really a club, more like a bar. He has six dancers and we all alternate nights. The place is always packed with men who drink too much and leer at us like we're a good cut of meat. It's smoky and smelly and I don't like it when they get grabby. But Justin makes sure that most of them tip well and treat us with respect."

"And he protects you. Makes you feel safe," Riley read from her notebook.

"Exactly. Why would I give it up when I make more money than half the people I know?"

"It's entirely your choice what you do for a career," Riley said. "You wouldn't happen to have a picture of Justin, do you? On your phone?"

"Sure, it's right here."

Chloe picked up her cell, opened her photos, and pointed him out to Riley. There were several, some in the dark smoky bar where his image wasn't clear, then one in front of the Kitty Cat Club in daylight, a big grin on his face. He had dark hair, dark eyes, and a thick mustache, not unattractive but not a showstopper.

"Do you mind forwarding that one to my email? He looks really happy there." And the full frontal would be helpful for an internet search if needed.

Chloe reluctantly sent it.

"You're being the best friend that you can be to Lacey, Chloe. I mean that."

"Thanks."

"No, thank you for being so cooperative. I'll let you know as soon as we find out anything."

"Yes, please do. I'm really shaken up right now." She started scratching her arms again. If not nerves, what else might cause scratching? An allergy. Or poison ivy. There was some three-pointed leaves in the shrubbery on the beach. Riley would go check it out.

Chapter Eleven

Riley slid into her Barbie-sized car, for the first time in her life half wishing she was shorter than her five foot four. Not forever, just when she was driving around with her knees up to her neck.

Bluetooth plugged in, she rejoiced that she had two bars of service! She was about to call the chief when he dialed her first. He must have the report already. Not already—wow, her interview with Chloe had taken an hour and it was now after three.

"Harper? Chief Barnes. Where are you?"

"Just leaving Lacey Killian's house. Spoke with Chloe, her best friend. Well? What did the coroner say?"

She heard him cough and could picture him running a hand over his thinning gray hair. The fact that he hadn't started gloating by now could only mean one thing. "I have the report right here."

"And?" Adrenaline washed through her followed by a healthy kick of satisfaction from being right. Not that she would gloat, but it felt damn fine to be good at her job against all odds.

"He agrees with your assessment. The bruising around the vic's neck and wrists could only come from a person's hands. Large. Male. Her face was too damaged to get any hints there, but she definitely took a nose-dive in addition to a beating. Now, don't get bigheaded over this."

She arched her brow at the phone, glad they weren't on video.

"Even though I'm the chief, I'm assigning you the lead on the case."

"Yes, Chief."

She stopped at a four-way stop sign and gave a fist pump, hitting the top of the Fiat. *Ouch!*

"What was that?"

"Nothing. I appreciate your faith in me." She thought about Chloe climbing the outer stairs of the lighthouse with her drunk friend in tow. That would explain her chipped nails, dirty feet, nervous behavior, *and* put her at the scene of the crime. But physically? It would be nearly impossible for a person of her build to toss a taller woman over the edge, intoxicated or not. Unless she had help. Could someone have already been up there, waiting for their arrival? Someone like Darren?

"Don't let me down, Harper."

Barnes was about to hang up when she stopped him. "Chief, are there surveillance cameras around the ferry? I'd like to see who was coming and going over the last week." Specifically, Justin DiCaprio. In Phoenix there were traffic cameras and surveillance cameras tucked all over the city.

"Nice idea. Ask Captain Wyatt if he has any footage of folks getting on and off. He'll have a registration log. I know there's a traffic cam set up at the dock. Not sure if it works—we've never had to use it before." She could practically hear his brain ticking. "I'd like to see it with you, if you don't mind?"

"Not at all. I'd be grateful for a second set of eyes." Had he just paid her a compliment? It must have hurt.

"There's another camera on the island, near Murphy's Marina."

"When were they installed? Do they get regular maintenance?" She turned her car toward the dock.

"After nine-eleven, security was beefed up everywhere. Guess they figured our island could harbor a few terrorists due to our proximity to Boston and Connecticut."

"Terrorists." The word made her shiver.

"Well, our island is safe from that kind of activity. Everybody knows everybody. You just concentrate on finding Lacey Killian's killer."

"She's got a lot of enemies right here on Sandpiper Bay. It won't be easy but I won't quit until I find out what happened to her."

"Good."

"Chief, I'm nearing the wharf now. Did you want to swing by the depot?"

"No. I think you can handle screening hours of video."

"Thanks." His sarcasm was starting to grow on her. "Any more good news, Chief? Like a camera near the lighthouse? An alibi for your boy, Darren?"

"That would be too easy, now, wouldn't it?" He actually laughed.

She smiled from the safety of her car. "So that's a no?"

"Good luck, Riley. You have good instincts, and I know this is what you wanted. Go after it."

"Will do." Was the chief mellowing toward her, or digging a ditch to bury her in?

She swung into the parking area across from the pier. No one was around except the old man with his chicken on his lap. Should she talk to him? She'd solved a case or two by questioning the nation's homeless. Once you broke the wall down by buying them a meal, they'd often remember the oddest things. And that's how crimes were solved.

Riley got out, locked the door, and crossed the street. The grizzled old man looked to be in his mid-seventies as she neared the porch. He bowed his head to avoid eye contact.

She stopped directly in front of his house but stayed on the sidewalk about six feet away. "Hello! I saw you here last week when my daughter, my mother, and I came in on the ferry."

He raised his tired, rheumy eyes from his chicken to flick a glance her way. "So?" His voice was a low rumble—scratchy, as if not used a lot.

"You don't need to talk, sir. I just wanted to introduce myself. I'm Officer Riley Harper." Moving forward, she gave him a warm, friendly smile and offered him a stick of gum, taking one herself. She was on the lawn below him. "Newest addition to the SBPD." She patted the sandpiper emblem on her uniform.

He unwrapped the foil, then slid the spearmint gum in his mouth, allowing his chicken to peck at the silver wrapper. It shone brightly as the midday sun hit it squarely.

"Are you here every day?"

He shrugged. "Depends."

"On the weather?"

"The weather, my mood, or if Harry gets sick."

The man had the perfect view of who would get on and off the ferry. Her only hope was that Justin's black and bushy mustache might be memorable. Otherwise, he was just average. It was worth a shot to see if her hunch was right. She knew for a fact that if you poked a man's pride, they got angry.

She edged to the steps. "Is Harry your chicken?"

He nodded, stroking his pet faster, his gum making smacking sounds as he shifted slightly to put more distance between them.

Riley pulled out her cell phone. "May I show you a picture of someone?"

He blinked at her, then reached for her phone.

"Hang on." She climbed to the porch and scrolled through her recent photos, then held up the clear picture of Justin DiCaprio.

The man shook his head.

Riley let him hold the phone himself. "Did you see this man come off the ferry in the past few days, or maybe get back on?" She knelt down and stroked the chicken to appear less threatening.

He rubbed his forehead. "Maybe, maybe not." He shrugged and looked down the pier where the ferry docked.

Riley sensed that she had his interest.

"I like it here." He didn't even glance at the phone. "Some folks offer money to pet Harry."

Now that was a hint as broad as daylight. "You scan the photos and I'll get my wallet." She chose a ten and handed it over. "Here you are. Don't want either of you going hungry."

His gray eyes lifted to hers. "He got on the ferry this morning. A woman was with him. She didn't get on."

Bingo! He'd been on the island when Lacey had been killed. "What time?"

He scratched his hairy chin. "After breakfast. Before lunch."

That was one way to tell time. "Hey! Are you hungry? I'm starved. Can I buy you a pizza from the pizza parlor?"

"They don't allow chickens inside the restaurant. I don't go anywhere without Harry."

"I can order it and bring it to you." Riley stood up and stretched her back. "Don't go anywhere. I'll be right back." She ran off to get a good look at the surveillance camera and saw the blinking red light telling her it was working. She looked from every angle to learn what the camera would see.

When she turned around to see what kind of pizza the old man would like, she was shocked to find that he'd disappeared.

Had she frightened him, or was he worried that speaking the truth to her might not have been his safest choice? She'd bet her brand-new snow boots that he knew more about this island and the people than the majority of residents did, and not a one would harm a hair on his head.

But a stranger? He might, if he believed the old man had seen more than he let on.

She dusted herself off and pulled hand sanitizer from her vest pocket to clean her hands. With or without the chicken man, she was determined to find the Italian restaurant Joan had recommended, as had Chief Barnes. She needed fuel to keep her going till dinner.

Riley stopped at the basket vendor and bought another basket from Melo, who cheerfully pointed her in the right direction. Five minutes later she noticed a neon sign that read Piazza Piper with a picture of the island's signature bird on it. She'd have a pie delivered to the old man.

It was quarter to four and her stomach was rumbling. She'd had a fritter that Nancy had brought this morning, then the slice of quiche while talking to Joan. No wonder she was ravenous.

Opening the door, she was surprised to see so few customers inside the large building. Pizza was universal. Two young couples, tourists she'd guess if their sunburned noses were anything to judge by, were seated near the window with a view of the dusty road and the beauty of the bay with the forest beyond.

The scent of tomato and garlic lured her inside. Her jaw dropped as she surveyed the interior space. No wonder the place came so highly recommended! Didn't matter what the food tasted like—the interior design was worth the trip. The walls were painted with a mural capturing the Amalfi coastline. Magnificent cliffs, the brilliant blue sea below, a shot of Positano.

It brought back her youth. The time she'd visited Italy with college friends after graduation. Before marriage, before police training, and before Kyra. She was glad for that time, but she knew that now she had so much more.

When she stopped gazing at the walls, her eyes swept toward the bar, where one guy sat alone. The back of his head looked familiar so when he turned around, she grinned and waved. He patted the chair beside him. Here was the second biggest gossip on the island. Hoping to glean some new information about Lacey, she strode over to join Coby, who had a plate of steaming pizza in front of him. She leaned on the counter.

"What are you doing here instead of minding your own bar? Your bartender told me you had someone quit." She glanced around, curious. "Better food?" A gorgeous woman with auburn hair laughed joyfully as she rounded a corner, depositing plates before the lucky diners by the window. "Or could it be that pretty waitress headed our way?"

Coby's cheeks flushed. "That's Maria Catalina, the owner. And yes, much better food." He lifted his slice of loaded pizza and took a large bite as if to prove it.

"Officer Harper! So, you finally come in!" Maria opened her arms and folded her into a big hug, as if they were old friends. Riley got a whiff of subtle carnation perfume and tomato sauce. "I have been hearing so much about this policewoman and does she come to see me? *No.* I am famous on this little strip of land and so is my pizza." Maria winked dark lashes. "If you hadn't come in today, *bella,* I was going to drive to your cabin and kidnap you and your family to share a meal."

"I'm a police officer and that would be a crime." Riley smiled warmly at the woman, charmed by her already. She had flowing auburn hair to her waist, a creamy clear complexion, and a loud voice. With her dancing eyes and her big laugh, Riley could clearly see her huge heart.

Coby made the unnecessary introductions and Maria gave him a boisterous peck on the cheek. "He's my most regular customer and tells everyone about this place. Every once in a while I reward him with an entire pizza pie. Not too often. Only when he pleases me."

Coby's neck turned red, and Riley gave him a curious look. What did he do to please this bighearted woman? The answer was obvious as was their affection. She had little doubt that the two of them were having an affair. She put Maria's age at closer to her own, while Coby was barely thirty. But why not?

"Maria, this interior is stunning. Did a local artist paint the murals for you?"

"Yes. The place was unpleasant inside, that's why I got it so cheap. I did the painting. You like?"

"I *love.* It's amazing." Riley had no artistry in any of her bones.

Her cheeks heated with color. "I think you and I will become very good friends. But first I must feed you. Here is a menu, but Coby knows it better than I."

"She's having what I'm having," Coby told his friend. "I never knew roasted eggplant could taste so good with pepperoni."

Maria laughed, brushed her hands on her curvy hips, and headed toward a sliding glass window that connected to the kitchen. "Hey, Will. We have our new lady of the law here. She wants the Coby special." She bobbed her head at something he said, then hips swaying, she waltzed back to the counter, poured half a glass of Miller Lite into a mug, and took a large sip.

"Riley, my new friend, may I offer you a drink? First one's on the house."

"I wish I could say yes, but I'm on duty." She didn't want to break the truce she and the chief had formed.

"Duty!" Maria snorted. "What do the police have to worry about here? We laugh, we love, we eat, and we drink. Chief Barnes cuts loose once in a while too, *cara*, I know. He and his wife Shelley can dance and sing."

Coby shot Maria a look. "Haven't you heard?"

"Heard what, my sweet man?" She raised her mug again to drink.

"A woman is dead. She was found in the water below the Sandpiper Bay Lighthouse." He cringed. "I know one of the paramedics. Too much partying and drinking, I suppose."

"When did this happen?" Maria brought her fingers to her throat. "How come I haven't heard?"

"We are keeping her identity under wraps until her family"—if she had any, Riley thought—"can be notified."

"I bet it's Lacey Killian." Coby said softly, watching Riley closely. "She was at the Lobster Pot last night with her red-haired friend and got really rowdy. Crazy girls and crazy night. Joan told me that poor Matty had to give them each a ticket." He turned to Maria. "This one sitting next to me is so nice that she let Lacey and her friend off with a warning when they were both topless in my bar."

"Who is Lacey?" Maria asked incredulously.

Riley gave Coby a kick under the bar counter.

Coby took a bite of pizza. "She used to live here but moved away to dance at a strip club. She's no good, trust me on that."

Riley was reminded of the anger between Coby and Lacey that Friday. But no...surely that was normal anger, not a prequel to killing her? She shook her head.

"Matty? Do you mean Officer Matthew Sniders?" She chuckled. "I can't wait to call him that."

Coby rested his elbow on the counter. "I heard it from Katie, and it cracks me up. Feel free to tease! I was in this morning trying to borrow one of her waitresses, and she told me all about how Lacey verbally attacked her. It was like she was jealous of Katie."

Maria sipped her brew.

"Chloe said that too when I talked with her earlier," Riley shared quietly. She wasn't confirming Lacey being the dead body.

"Katie said that Lacey used to be their ringleader, taunting the other kids, making them do weird things that these nice kids would never think to do."

"What kind of things?" Maria sniffed. "Hold it! Your pizza is ready, I'll be right back."

Coby had finished his pie and was sucking back the last of his beer. "Don't know what they got up to, but it was dangerous, or so Katie implied."

Riley tasted her pizza, moaned, then wiped her mouth. "I don't get it. The girl might be bad, but she's not Charles Manson. How could she control them? Why wouldn't they just do the right thing, walk away and tell their parents?"

"I've been here for twenty years and people on the island protect their own and don't snitch." Maria shrugged in a c'est la vie manner. "How's the pizza?"

Riley felt a punch to her gut when Marie used the word snitch. Did the whole island know? Were they talking about her constantly?

She swallowed hard, no longer enjoying the friendship or the food.

"Maria, could I box this to go? I also need to order two different pizzas. One for the man with the chicken across from the depot, probably a cheese? And another large whatever you want to make for me to take home this evening. It's been an exhausting day." And she still had a lot of work to do. Murders didn't get solved from nine to five.

"Of course! There's a lull between now and the dinner crowd. Will can fix you up something in no time, or better yet, when my help gets here around five, I could deliver it to your home, still warm from the oven."

"I can't ask you to do that."

"I'm happy to do it. Get out of here for a half hour, meet your mother and daughter, and besides, I live within two blocks of you."

"Well, if you're sure..."

"Wouldn't say it if I didn't mean it."

Had Maria meant to call her a snitch?

Riley cleared her throat. "I'll take a large cheese then, to go." She boxed her pizza, paid her bill, and wasn't surprised when Coby walked her outside to the parking lot. Her car was at the depot.

"I know you can't tell me if the person at the morgue is Lacey, but I know it is, from my paramedic friend. The snake tattoo? Just be careful, all right? She has a lot of enemies."

"Lacey *had* a lot of enemies," Riley corrected. "She's dead and it is my duty to find out who killed her."

Chapter Twelve

Riley walked the few blocks from Piazza Piper to the ferry depot and put her extra-large slice of pizza in its cardboard box on the seat next to her. *Snitch. Rat. Backstabber.* She'd heard it all after she'd testified, but it had taken her by surprise just now to hear the word from Maria.

To be fair, it might not have been directed at her, but she was sensitive to the word. The chicken man wasn't on his porch, so she left the cheese pizza on his chair.

Her phone rang. "Officer Harper."

"This is Barnes. I talked to Captain Wyatt and let him know you might be stopping by. This is *your* case, and if you think the video is worth seeing, then I support that."

Riley didn't need any more encouragement and strode across the street, directly to the ferry office. At quarter past four in the afternoon, the depot was quiet when she entered. It reminded her of a Greyhound bus station but instead of multiple terminals to buy tickets, there was a single booth.

"Hiya," Captain Wyatt said.

Riley raised her hand in a wave. "Hi. I'm Officer Riley Harper. I don't know if you remember me?"

"The uniform gave it away," he drawled. "I'm Captain Wyatt Michaud." He winked. "This is the first I've seen you wear it—when we met before, you were traveling with your mother and your daughter."

"Good memory!"

"What can I do for you?"

She smiled—his eyes twinkled, blue orbs with an overhang of bushy white brows, inviting a laugh. The red cheeks and spider-veined skin over his nose suggested a lot of time in the harsh weather. "I noticed your surveillance camera outside. I'd like to see the footage from this morning's outbound ferry trips."

He tapped his nose sagely. "This got to do with the dead girl at the lighthouse?"

"Could be." Riley shrugged and leaned her elbow on the chest-high counter that was four feet in width. "I can't say for sure."

"I heard from a friend of a friend that it's the Killian girl. I've known her since she first was taken in by her grandparents, God rest their souls."

Riley nodded for him to continue. Seems she'd get information without a bribe this time. Maybe because of the chief's "friendly" call?

"Her folks passed in a car accident when she was around eight or nine. Skinny little thing. I heard she left home to be a stripper." The captain shook his head, his gaze sad.

"Exotic dancer in Portland." Riley shifted. "Did Justin DiCaprio get a ride to the mainland this morning?"

Wyatt turned to his computer and tapped a few buttons. "Nobody by that name." He scanned the list.

"Is there a way he might have snuck on? The man across the street with the chicken said he saw him board."

Wyatt guffawed and smacked his side of the counter. "Chicken man. That's old Ollie Pelletier and he's been a fixture around here since *I* was a kid."

"Has he always had a chicken for a pet?"

"That's no pet, Officer Harper. He gets a new one every three months after the older one goes into the stew pot."

Riley sucked in a breath. "Are you kidding?"

"Nope. He says all of the attention makes them fat and juicy." Captain Wyatt waggled a bushy brow. "Not that I've ever been invited to Sunday dinner. Just what he tells me."

Riley looped her thumbs over her belt not sure if she was being had again. Poke at the new officer and see how gullible she is?

"I'd like to see the footage from this morning, if you have it."

"Oh, ayuh. I can do that." He glanced at the clock. "Thing is, I'm captaining the ferry at four thirty, and I'll need to close up shop. My second mate Deke is out sick today." He tipped up his hands to mime drinking. "Bottle flu. Happens after every payday."

"Oh...does he need, er, help?"

"Nah. He's a good kid—twenty-eight days out of thirty." Captain Wyatt boomed his laugh and it echoed in the empty depot. Assorted chairs waited forlornly for paying customers.

Riley knew from her own experience what a madhouse this place could be right before leaving to the mainland, and upon arrival. It was possible that Justin might have crept aboard, especially if Captain Wyatt was short-handed.

"The video? I'd fill out a voucher so that I could take it to the station for a thorough examination."

Captain Wyatt nodded. "Sure, sure. To be official." He peered at her. "I like the look of you though, Officer Harper."

What could she say to that? Riley tapped the counter to stay on topic. "What about last week?" Lacey had come in on Friday and it might be important to see if Justin was on that ferry. "Can you see if Justin DiCaprio was on that crossing, the day Lacey arrived?"

Captain Wyatt did a search. "Nothing. Nobody by that last name. Sorry."

"Do you have any Justin?"

He blew out a breath and gave her a look to let her know she was starting to get on his nerves. "Lemme see."

Riley leaned closer to look into his office though she couldn't see the manifest.

"Yep. Got a Justin Smith leaving this morning."

She pulled out her cell phone to show him Justin's picture. "Do you recognize him?"

Captain Wyatt nodded. "That's him. DiCaprio. What a joke."

Riley sighed. The owner of the Kitty Cat Club thought highly of himself. "Do you mind checking to see if Justin Smith arrived the same day as Lacey and her friend, Chloe?"

He located the file on his computer and ran his finger down the list. "Yep. Lacey Killian. Chloe Risk. No Justin."

"Is this the only way of getting to the mainland?"

"It's the safest and most reliable. You could hire a fishing boat I suppose. Talk to Hunter Jackson down at the harbor if this doesn't pan out. Trustworthy and probably the best fisherman we've got."

She bit the inside of her lip, then gave a nod. "I'd like to see the footage from the day that Lacey arrived in Sandpiper Bay too."

"No worries. So long as you get it back to me."

In Phoenix there had been official forms for removing the tape off property when you took something back to the station. She'd have to ask Nancy if there was something like that here.

"I will. In the meantime, I can write the borrowing of the tape down on a piece of paper."

Captain Wyatt skewered her with his shrewd gaze. "You look trustworthy. Gimme a sec and I'll get it for you. This morning, and last Wednesday. We do a daily record and keep them for a month, then reuse the old tape. It came in handy last year when we discovered a woman from the mainland coming over twice a week and leaving with more than what she'd arrived with, if you get my meaning. Me and Deke caught her red-handed."

"Good for you! What did the chief say?"

"Chief Barnes escorted her home where the officers there arrested her. Sandpiper Bay is a good place."

Riley thought of Lacey's battered body, dead on the rocks, and doubt must have shown on her face.

Captain Wyatt flushed. "Usually."

She nodded. "Let's find out what happened to Lacey. I do appreciate your help. Captain? Wyatt? What do you like to be called?"

"Most folks around here call me Captain. I'd be pleased if you'd do the same."

The small token of acceptance warmed her, especially after her overreaction at Maria's restaurant. The woman was too bighearted to be cruel.

"Thank you."

He hustled into a back office that had been closed, leaving it open a crack behind him. Riley noticed overflowing shelves and an old video recorder that wasn't from this century. He shuffled papers off a desk, then opened a drawer.

Not the tidiest system, but if it worked... If only Kyra was sixteen, she might apply for a job here.

He returned with two tapes in triumph. "Here you go, Officer. I hope this helps with uncovering what happened to Lacey. She might not have been a good girl, but I'll never forget how scared she was, moving in with her grandparents so young. She had a hard beginning."

"Did she get on well with her grandparents?"

"Ah, they doted on her, to make up for her loss. Maybe they spoiled her." He lifted a thick shoulder, a fisherman and ferry captain to his core. "Can't blame 'em, but it's a shame all around."

"I agree." Riley filled out a receipt on her spiral tablet in her pocket and handed it to Wyatt. He took it and slid the tapes across the counter in exchange.

"Fair sailing to you, Officer Harper."

She smiled. "And to you."

She got into her car, cheese and tomato sauce making her tummy growl. With the success of her mission, her stomach had unknotted, and she could eat the pizza slice she hadn't been able to finish at the pizza parlor.

Ollie the chicken man remained out of sight. Was he stewing Harry right now?

She opened the box of her pizza and bit into the cheesy deliciousness, determined to keep positive thoughts until the slice was finished. Eggplant and pepperoni. Who knew?

Riley arrived at the station with a clearer head. She brought the tapes from the ferry office to the open workspaces partially shielded behind Nancy's desk, and placed them by the evidence bags.

Nancy greeted her with a smile. "Chief had an emergency at home, the plumbing or some dang thing. But Matthew's in his office if you want to knock and let him know you're back."

"Thanks."

The receptionist's phone rang and she answered, tuning Riley out. Riley passed her own office and tapped on Matthew's. His door was partially open and he grinned when he saw her.

"Success with the tapes at the depot? The chief mentioned you'd had a great idea about viewing those and the traffic cams."

"I got two tapes." She entered and leaned against his desk. She thought about teasing him with his nickname Matty but decided to wait until she knew him better. "This morning's footage, to double-check a witness's claim. I also want to see the day that Lacey came across from the mainland."

"What are you thinking?" Matthew sat back in his chair, his elbow on the armrest. He looked much more rested than he had this morning, she was glad to see.

"Justin DiCaprio is the owner of the strip club where Lacey and Chloe work. Well, worked. Chloe raved about what a great boss he is and that he and Lacey had had a thing."

"Isn't that a perk for the boss to have his pick of the girls?"

Riley snorted in surprise. "Well, I just don't know, Matthew. It's not my area of expertise."

He blushed. "I like crime dramas on television. Not a real-life fan of the clubs."

Riley stopped teasing the poor kid, but it was so easy! "I found out from the chicken man, I mean, Ollie Pelletier, that he saw Justin get on board the ferry this morning. Only Captain Wyatt didn't have a Justin DiCaprio on the manifest. His real name is Justin Smith and Chloe told me that he took the breakup between him and Lacey very hard."

"Excellent work!" Matthew rose fluidly and gestured to the hall and the back tables. "Let's see what you've got."

"These videos came from an ancient machine." In Phoenix things had been slick and modernized.

"We have an ancient video player," Matthew assured her.

"Thank heaven! We need to prove that Justin was here on the island and that he left. Chloe was acting sketchy about it, but she might be protecting her boss. I mean, now that Lacey is dead, Chloe will have to return to the strip club. She and Lacey were going to sell the cabin and move to Vegas, but that plan is dead now."

"Did you believe her?"

"Yeah. Why would she kill Lacey? Lacey was her ticket to the glitz and glamour of Las Vegas. Then again Ollie said he saw a girl with Justin this morning, but the girl didn't get on the ferry. Could be Chloe, helping Justin get away?"

"So many possibilities." Matthew reached across the table to a shelf full of electronics from the same decade as the tapes.

Unbelievable to be stuck in the past, but it was working in her favor.

Matthew got the machine powered on and slid in the tape.

"This is today," Riley said. "The captain told me they do a twenty-four-hour recording."

"That makes it easy, huh?" He crossed his arms and leaned his hip against the desk.

Riley brought out her phone and showed Matthew the picture of Justin she'd gotten from Chloe's phone. "Average height. Brown hair, bushy mustache. Good-looking in a slick way."

Matthew studied the image closely. "Never seen him before."

"What about the night you went to the Lobster Pot because Lacey was fighting with Katie? He might have been around then. I got the feeling from Chloe that Lacey was jealous of Katie. Do you know why?"

Mathew's lower lip jutted. "Nope. And this Justin guy wasn't around. It was Katie and Carter, and Chloe and Lacey. Nobody else."

Riley watched the blurred video. Commuters all dressed for jobs on the mainland came in waves at six, seven, eight, and nine, but by ten things had slowed. Between breakfast and lunch, Ollie had said. Who needed a clock?

"Can't believe that someone I knew is dead," Matthew murmured sadly.

He and Lacey were around the same age. Same as Katie. And Coby. Late twenties. "I'm sorry, Matthew."

He grimaced. "What's worse?"

"What?" Riley couldn't think of anything worse than death.

"That someone I know might have killed her." His voice shook and it was all Riley could do to not give him a hug.

Chapter Thirteen

Riley patted Matthew's upper arm in commiseration rather than risk breaking a stupid rule. Her luck, Chief would walk in while she was consoling Matthew and he'd have grounds to fire her.

"Maybe not. Let's find out for sure. Captain Wyatt told me that Lacey's parents are dead too, which means we can probably release the news that it was Lacey in the ocean this morning. Although funnily enough, everyone seems to know anyway." She looked from Matthew to the video screen. "Stop!"

Matthew pressed the button and the frame froze. "This him?"

"Yes." She compared the photo on her phone to the blurred image. "Justin Smith aka Justin DiCaprio."

"All right—what next?"

"We know where he works in Portland because he owns the Kitty Cat strip club. Let's run a background check on him. He is definitely a person of interest. Unless he's got a solid alibi, I want him back on this island."

"You got it."

"Speaking of alibis...did you ever talk to Darren Williams?"

"Yeah. He let me in and wanted to apologize for being so out of it earlier. Finding Lacey's body came as a shock, he told me."

He remained a person of interest until Riley could clear him. "You got a picture of his knuckles?"

"Yep. He says that he is on the gallery deck every day, and he might have scraped his hand along the wall."

How convenient! "Very interesting, don't you think?"

Matthew shrugged, his expression doubtful. "I don't know, Riley. He took something to sleep after the argument because he was so wired up."

"So he claims."

"What've you got against Darren?" Matthew challenged.

And why did Barnes and Matthew have a blind spot for the veteran? "I have no agenda other than trying to find out how Lacey Killian died."

Matthew sighed. "Darren is a good guy."

"Still, find out what he takes for sleeping pills. Is it prescription? Mixed with drinking it could change a decent human into a monster." She thought of her ex, Fraser, when he got drunk. She hid her face to look at the video screen.

"I'll check." His tone told her he didn't like it.

Rosita arrived with a case of fizzy water for the back room and called a greeting as she passed them toward the kitchen.

Riley wondered why the civilian officer was there. Wasn't her schedule on a Tuesday? Maybe she was curious about the first murder case in Sandpiper Bay in a long time. Couldn't blame her there.

Or maybe Rosita was just a nice woman and Riley needed to not be so paranoid. Rosita was back in moments with lemon waters for all of them, cracking hers with a satisfying hiss before she sipped. "How's it going? I've been dying to know what's happening."

Riley laughed at herself for making a big deal of nothing. If Rosita was really interested in a full-time position at the station, then Riley would help her get it somehow. They were barely acquaintances but that would change over the next year.

"Thanks!"

"Welcome. Did you find out more about what happened to Lacey?" She set the can on the table and studied the frozen screen with Justin's blurry image. "Hey, I saw that guy this morning."

"On the ferry?" Riley asked. That would make two witnesses to place Justin at the depot.

"No, no." Rosita shook her head and gripped Riley's wrist. "He was leaving Lacey's house."

"That can't be right," Riley mused. "Chloe was very insistent that she hadn't seen her boss from the club, Justin. Was he outside the house, maybe?"

Matthew crossed his arms. "You said Chloe was acting cagey—maybe she was sheltering him the whole time."

Riley gritted her teeth, feeling duped. "Guess I'll be going back to Lacey's. Why on earth would she lie about him being there?" *Unless they were in this together.*

Chief Barnes came in through the back with a cardboard box filled with Lacey's things. The red dress. Heels. "Sorry I had to run out, but here's more for the evidence log. How's it going?"

Riley had so many questions, but she would follow each thread until she had answers. "Did Lacey have a cell phone?" Riley asked.

"Not with her clothes, no." The chief rested the box on the edge of the long table. "I wouldn't count on finding it. It would be too easy to destroy it or toss it in the ocean."

Riley nodded.

Why the folded dress? Was Justin a neat freak? Riley quickly brought the chief up to speed regarding Justin. "We need to question him further. See if he's got an alibi." She had a sneaking feeling that Chloe knew exactly where he'd been.

"I'll do that, if you'd like. I have an appointment in Portland tomorrow. I can drop in at the club. Do some recon."

"Really, Chief?" Riley waited for a snide remark, but the infuriating man simply shrugged. "Thanks."

"Seems like you're doing good work here. Keep it up. Who else is doing what?"

Riley pointed to Matthew. "Matthew is going to run a background check today on Justin—and if you meet him personally, we should get a vibe. He's either under Smith or DiCaprio. I plan on going back to Lacey's house to talk to Chloe. Uh, she was sure itchy and I noticed red blotches on her arm. Is there poison ivy around here?"

"Oh, it's everywhere," Rosita said. "It's really adapted to Maine weather and grows from the forest to the beach."

"Is it in the bushes around the lighthouse?"

Matthew arched a brow. "Why do you ask?"

"She was scratching like crazy. It would place Chloe at the beach and rocks, possibly with Lacey, even though she said she hadn't seen Lacey after midnight."

"Interesting." Chief Barnes took a manila file from the top of the box and opened it. "The medical examiner estimates the time of death between midnight and two a.m. The cool temperature of the Atlantic had kept her body chilled which slowed lividity."

"It's my opinion that Chloe is likely lying," Riley said with dismay. "She's lied about seeing Justin."

Matthew grabbed a tablet of paper and his pen and jotted down notes. "I can check on the poison ivy. I hate that stuff."

"It doesn't bother me," Nancy said between a break of not answering phones. Most folks wanted to know if the SPPD had caught the Lighthouse Killer yet. "But my sister? We had to bathe her in calamine lotion as a kid."

Riley picked up her can of lemon water. "I'm going to head over to Lacey's. I'd hate for Chloe to do a disappearing act." She turned to the chief. "Who will get Lacey's house now?"

"Don't know. She doesn't have any other living kin. Not even a cousin. Search to see if she had a will while you're in the house, all right?" Chief asked.

"I will." Riley braced herself for a tough interview. How to get past Chloe's guard? "Nancy, did you say that calamine lotion helped your sister? I can buy some for Chloe as a reason for stopping by."

"Smart. Get her to open up to you." Rosita bobbed her head with approval. Another small sign of acceptance?

Riley left the station at quarter to five. She stopped at the General Store and bought a small pink bottle of lotion guaranteed to ease the itch of poison ivy.

Now, she told herself, think of this as dealing with Kyra when she's in a bad mood. Tread softly to get answers.

The woman had lied to Riley which was a pet peeve. Not the first time a possible suspect hadn't told her the truth and there'd be plenty more. She just had to suck it up.

She parked in front of the cute cottage once owned by Lacey's grandparents, wondering what would happen to it now.

Riley saw the curtain move as Chloe peeked out. She exited the Fiat, lifted the bag, and waved. No way would she let the woman try to act like she wasn't there.

For the second time that day, Chloe reluctantly opened the front door and ushered Riley inside Lacey's house. This time she was dressed in short shorts and a low-cut tee.

The home wasn't really Lacey's though and still had the furniture and pictures of the older couple. Riley had another agenda now that she inside again: to find a will and to find evidence that Justin had been there earlier.

Lacey had been the Killians' pride and joy and her photo from when she'd been around sixteen was centered above the fireplace.

She'd been pretty, but sly. Her battered face had been unrecognizable when Riley had first seen her in the water. If Lacey hadn't gotten those injuries from landing on the rocks, then that type of beating spoke of rage.

Riley had thought that Chloe didn't have a reason to want Lacey out of the way—but what if Chloe wanted to take her best friend's man? And cabin on the beach? To heck with Vegas for a sure deal in Portland.

She smiled and offered the brown paper bag. "I brought you some lotion for your rash. I felt so bad for you when I left. You were just so itchy!"

The woman peered inside the bag. "Oh. Well. That's nice. I took some Benadryl that I found in the medicine cabinet. One thing about old people—they sure got lots of medication around. Nothing *good* though." She chuckled.

Riley kept her smile in place. "Did it help with the rash?" She looked at Chloe's arm.

The woman held it out. Only small red bumps remained.

"Oh, that's still there," Riley said, playing it up. "You better put the lotion on. That's poison ivy."

"*What?*"

"Yes. I couldn't believe it. Did you know it grows around the lighthouse?" And all over the island, unfortunately.

Chloe dropped the bag to the coffee table. "Can't be what I have then." Her glance skittered from Riley to the back door. "Is that why you're here?"

Rather than go on the attack, Riley shrugged and took a seat at the small kitchenette.

If Chloe tried to make a run for it, Riley was in position for either door. "I'd sure love a bottle of water, if you still have one. I appreciate the picture of Justin from earlier. He was on the ferry this morning. We just missed him."

Chloe's shoulders relaxed and she went into the kitchen and opened the fridge, getting two bottles of water. "That's all right. He didn't have anything to do with what happened to Lacey."

"How can you be so sure?"

Chloe uncapped the bottle and sat opposite Riley, her lip quivering. The girl was close to cracking. "I just am."

Riley scanned the kitchen. Three coffee mugs were in the sink, something she'd dismissed before, attributing the clutter to messy housekeeping. "He was here this morning?" She gestured toward the stainless-steel sink.

Her eyes widened and she looked behind her. "How do you know?"

"I also know," Riley dragged out, "that his name is an alias."

"A what?" Chloe gave Riley her full attention.

"DiCaprio isn't his real name." She tapped the table. "As you already know, I can tell. He spent the night here."

She waited for Chloe to give a sign of acknowledgement. Color raced up her throat. Good enough for Riley. "You weren't such a great friend to Lacey, were you?"

"I don't know what you mean," she trailed off.

Riley hoped she was right as she said, "Sleeping with Justin behind her back."

Chloe gulped her water, her eyes flickering.

"Did Lacey find out? Is that why you lured her to the lighthouse? Did you push her off, Chloe, or did Justin do it?"

"Stop it!" She rubbed the rash on her arms and then her leg.

"I know that the poison ivy you got into grows right around where her clothes were found."

"Listen. It doesn't matter now—Lacey is gone. Yes, I was hooking up with Justin. So what? Lacey wanted to move from where we make decent money to start over in Vegas. The girls there are real pros."

Riley narrowed her gaze at the crying young lady. "So you feared you wouldn't be up to the competition."

She sniffed and wiped her nose with the back of her hand. "You don't have to be mean about it."

Really? *Mean?* How childish. "Did you push Lacey, your best friend, over the rail of the lighthouse to land on the rocks?"

"No!" she screeched. "I didn't do that. Neither did Justin. Lacey ran off to be weird in the moonlight and I stayed here. With Justin."

"You slept together here? Ballsy." Some people had no shame. "What if she came back? Or had she and that's why you...?" It would be a motive as old as time. "Do you know where she kept her business papers...the deed to the house?"

"Her grandparents' desk." Chloe crossed her arms defensively. "I only know because she'd found it to sell the place—I didn't touch anything!"

Riley went into the grandparents' room where an old-fashioned metal box with a clasp sat on the desktop. Chloe and Justin'd had access to it. She lifted the top and shuffled through the yellowed papers. "Everything is here?"

Chloe sniffled. "Yeah. I was going to tell Lacey today that I didn't want to go to Vegas. I was going to stay here with Justin."

Riley brought the box to the kitchen table and shook her head. "In Lacey's house? Were you hoping that nobody would notice that she was gone?"

"Not this house. My apartment in Portland." Chloe eyed the geese pattern on the wall in the kitchen. "This place is ancient. I don't blame Lacey for wanting out."

Chloe started to cry harder and put a chipped purple thumbnail to her lower lip.

"So. Why should I believe you? You lied to me this morning." Riley leaned her elbow on the table, not the least bit empathetic to her tears.

"I know it makes us look guilty, but we didn't do it. Justin was with me. I was with him." Chloe nodded. "We can vouch for each other."

"You both have a reason to want Lacey out of the way. Maybe Justin killed her for leaving and shaming him. He could have followed her, full of rage. Or you knew that he still loved her and not you. You went along, believing you could step into her shoes." She tsked her tongue.

"No. No. I can prove that he loved me. We were here together." Chloe pulled out her phone and gave Riley information about their location, with a time stamp on the texts, way more than Riley wanted to know. Sexual positions, selfies in the bedroom.

Riley didn't know a person could get a tattoo there. *Ugh*. "Don't leave Sandpiper Bay, all right? I want you to stick around for a few days until we discover what happened to Lacey."

Chloe looked around the small cottage with a shiver. "I don't want to be here. I want to be with Justin," she whined.

Riley stood and picked up the metal box—all that remained of the Killians. "I think you owe it to Lacey, Chloe, for messing with Justin behind her back. If you didn't have anything to do with her death, then prove it by sticking around. Only guilty people run."

Her eyes glittered. "Did you just use a guilt trip on me?"

"Did it work?" Riley shrugged.

Chloe exhaled and pulled the bottle of calamine lotion from the bag, not answering Riley. "This is really supposed to help?"

"An oatmeal bath, and the lotion twice a day."

"You sound like my mom."

Riley's heart softened a tiny bit. "Are you still in touch with her?"

Chloe shook her head. "She doesn't approve of my lifestyle."

Riley stopped herself from giving advice, but just barely. The girl could be a killer or an accomplice, as well as a lousy friend.

"Take care, and don't leave the island," she said on her way out. Riley walked around the perimeter of the property and noted the ivy growing up the side of the pine trees. Three points. This stuff grew all over the island, Rosita said.

She drove back to the station with the heavy knowledge that Chloe and Justin had been filming themselves having sex in Lacey's bedroom. *Jerks*. Lacey had died between midnight and two in the morning, during their romp. It proved they were indecent human beings, but it didn't prove murder.

So who had Lacey been with? She'd put the pressure herself on Darren Williams until he confessed all.

Chapter Fourteen

It was after six by the time she reached the unlit station. When she went in, Nancy and Rosita were gone, as was the chief, but Matthew was still working in his office.

She waved to him and went into hers to call home.

"Hey, hon," her mom sang as she answered the phone. "On your way?"

"Not yet. I called to tell you that I was running late, and I will be a bit *more* late, and I've ordered dinner from the Piazza Piper to be delivered to the house."

Susan must have her on speaker because Riley heard Kyra cheer in the background. "Did Mom say pizza?"

"Tell Kyra that it's Italian, and I don't know exactly what Maria, the owner, will be bringing by. I'll try to get home within the hour."

Her mom gave a rare huff. "I was in the process of making a chicken pot pie from scratch, but I've got a feeling Kyra and I will enjoy this better."

"Can you save the pie for tomorrow, Mom? Or will it get ruined? If not, we'll have your dinner and save the Italian for tomorrow." Riley didn't want to take her mother's being home with Kyra for granted.

"Please, Nana?" Kyra asked in a sweet voice. "Your chicken pot pie is delicious, but this is something new."

"I love your pot pie too, Mom. I should have called earlier, but I've been working on a case." She hadn't told her family about the murdered stripper. She preferred to keep the ugly parts of her job at the department.

"Is this about the dead girl at the lighthouse?" Susan's tone held concern.

"How did you hear about that? I thought you both were home all day!"

"We went to buy crafts for a birdhouse," Kyra said, sounding as if she'd joined Susan in the kitchen. "And it was all the lady at the market talked about."

Riley hadn't met a woman at the market yet, just a man, Chet or Charlie, she couldn't remember. "What were they say...never mind, tell me when I get there." Small island living was not the same as big city and she would need to adjust her thinking.

"Is the lighthouse really a place where jilted lovers jump into the sea?" Kyra asked.

Riley burst out laughing at her tween daughter using such an archaic term. "Later. Save me a plate of whatever Maria delivers, all right? She's a character and you both are gonna adore her."

"Weird, Mom. Hey, I think that's the door!" Kyra raced off so loudly Riley heard her sneakers pound the wood floors of the kitchen.

Susan laughed. "I should go. I'm about done with the pie. It'll be great tomorrow."

"Thanks, Mom. I'm going to stop by the lighthouse on my way home, so it'll be an hour or so—don't wait for me but save me a plate. Love you both!" She ended the call with a grin. They'd only been here just over a week but already it was starting to feel like home. If only Kyra could meet some friends, and her mom too, the year would go by fast.

Riley logged in her conversation with Chloe, then knocked on Matthew's door to say goodbye, but he was gone too so she locked up the station. It hit her how much smaller this place was compared to her old precinct. Maybe that wasn't a bad thing.

The sun had not completely set by the time she arrived at the Sandpiper Bay Lighthouse. It was open until seven, and it was now quarter till. She was one of three cars in the small parking lot, but she didn't see anybody else around.

Keeping her eye out for Darren, she descended the steep and narrow path down the hillside to the beach below. The tide was out, and she was able to walk to the outcropping of rocks where she'd examined Lacey's body, the water to her ankles. Sea spray had destroyed any blood or fluids. From her vantage point, she turned back around to face the lighthouse.

The incline had to be a hundred feet. Ocean water lapped at her ankles and she decided that she had time to run up to the gallery deck on the lighthouse for another poke around. She ascended the hill using the smaller trail that led directly to the metal staircase of the lighthouse.

Riley reached the top of the cliff and paused to take in her surroundings. Pine and evergreen trees formed a barrier to her left and behind her, the sea vast and mysterious before her, the lighthouse at her back to the right, which blocked the parking lot. She hadn't seen another person despite the other cars.

It was a spectacular view as the sun sank into the choppy cove. It you listened past the surf, she could hear squirrels running up the fir trees. The gulls squawking.

A branch crunched in the near dark and Riley's pulse skipped a warning.

She spun around, her heart thundering.

Darren held a rifle in his hands, loose and casual, as if holding a weapon was ever anything less than dangerous, especially in a soldier's grip.

Had *he* killed Lacey? Riley raised her chin. Yes, she wore her Kevlar vest but that wouldn't stop a trained veteran, a man suffering the effects of PTSD. She held her hands out to show him that she was unarmed.

"Darren. Just the man I came to see." She gave a brief smile that he didn't return.

"What are you doing here?" He stroked the rifle as if it were a cat. Soothing pats down the length of the gun. "Visiting hours are over."

That would make it just seven in the evening. "Like I said, I was hoping to speak with you for a few moments."

His eyes narrowed and he placed the rifle over his shoulder in a drill position, the muzzle pointing upward. Was this a routine drill for him—making sure the last visitor had gone? Did he see this as defense of his home? After visiting hours, nobody should be allowed to trespass. In his mind, perhaps this was *his* lighthouse.

"I already talked to Sniders."

"I just spoke with Chloe Risk, Lacey's best friend. You know her?"

He studied her with a blank expression that made her blood chill. "No."

Living alone in a dark lighthouse, fearful of people, licensed to carry a rifle...she imagined the other night. Perhaps he'd been startled by the noises from up above. Awakened after midnight, listening to the sound of a drunk woman either arguing with someone or laughing, having fun. Lacey's companions hadn't been Chloe or Justin. Darren, if Riley set aside the idea that he was guilty, might give her a clue as to who Lacey had been with.

Chloe had told Riley that Lacey "knew" most of the guys on this island, including Darren. What if Darren had been jealous? Reacted in anger? For Lacey to have been thrown or beaten the way she had, her skull crushed, showed deep rage.

Darren remained still as a scout on patrol, rifle at his shoulder, black wool cap on his head.

"Darren, I don't mean you any harm." She maintained eye contact. Kept her voice modulated. "I just have a few more questions about what you saw or heard the other night when Lacey was killed."

"Told Sniders everything I knew."

"According to Officer Sniders, you were fast asleep when Lacey Killian clambered up the metal stairway to reach the platform that encircles the lantern room. That had to have been jarring for you to wake up to."

He tugged his wool cap lower to cover his ears. "No, ma'am."

He had heard something! Riley kept her voice controlled. "I don't think Lacey was alone. This is important. Did you hear anything? A noise, a scream, the sound of a scuffle?"

His jaw clenched. "No, ma'am."

"Darren, you are in a unique position to help me discover who killed Lacey." She gave him a brief smile. "You live here. This is your domain. She trespassed. It wouldn't be against the law to protect your property."

Darren took a few steps back and rested his hand on the butt of the rifle. She knew that he could fire that weapon in an instant. She swallowed hard. Fear slithered over her skin like a snake.

Her mom knew that she was going to stop by the lighthouse, but nobody else did. A part of her wished she'd told Matthew, but he'd been gone already. It was strange he hadn't said goodbye.

"You should go." Darren gestured with the rifle to the lighthouse behind him and the parking lot she couldn't see.

"I heard that you knew Lacey when she lived here as a kid. A teenager. You were an item, weren't you?" How far could she push without getting a rifle down her throat? "Did she dump you? Break your heart?" Heart thudding, she kept the heat on. If she pushed a little more, would Darren give her the information she wanted? Better yet, confess? "By not talking with me, you make yourself look guilty. Let me help."

"Leave!" His dark eyes flashed with fury.

"Listen, I don't have to be your adversary." Riley skirted around him so that her back wasn't to the cliff and the water. "What if you were having a nightmare? You might have thought there was an enemy at your door! No jury would convict you of protecting your home." Softening her voice, she whispered, "Please, Darren, tell me what you heard."

His throat worked as he gulped, his gaze flicking to the water, to her gun at her hip, to the lighthouse. His grip tightened on the rifle though he didn't point it at her. He was in sentinel mode. Protect.

"Darren?" She spoke softly instead of running for her car. "I don't think Lacey jumped from the gallery deck. She had bruises around her wrists."

He swallowed again, then looked at Riley in the twilight. "I found her that morning. I called the station. I could tell"—he blinked rapidly—"that she was dead."

"Did you touch her body to confirm that?"

He stared at her, his gaze hardening. "You know she was in the water. How could I have?"

Riley realized she'd just tripped up. *Dang it.* "Officer Sniders told me you were fast asleep because you take sleeping pills. Is that all you take?"

"Melatonin. So? Sometimes it works, sometimes it doesn't." Darren's head tilted and his knuckles cracked as he tightened his hold on the rifle. "You can get that over the counter, *Officer.*"

His defenses rose like an all-over body shield and she needed to back off. "Thanks for answering my questions. If you think of anything else, please call the chief or your friend *Matty.*" Riley turned to leave. "Take care."

Darren lowered the rifle so that it was loose at his hip. "You too, Officer." He adjusted his wool cap, his eyes on her like a target. "Seen your mama and daughter around. Cute kid." He melted backward into the pine trees like a shadow.

"Hey! Come back here!" Had that been a threat? Cold sweat trickled down her spine, and Riley jumped into her car. She was a mix of furious and scared, not how she wanted to go home. How dare he say that?

Torn, she thought of dialing the chief. And tell him what, exactly? That his pet soldier had just threatened her?

Had it been a threat?

She banged her palm to the steering wheel, then dialed Matthew.

"Officer Sniders," he said.

"Mathew? Riley." She breathed in a deep yoga breath to calm the hell down.

"Miss me already? You were on the phone when I left so I didn't say goodbye. What's up?"

"Darren might have killed Lacey," she blurted. "Hero hidden in plain sight."

"Whoa! Where are you now?" Matthew asked. "I'm just sitting down for a cup of soup at the Lobster Pot. Join me."

It was tempting, but she had dinner with her family waiting at home. She couldn't be jittery or upset with them, which meant spilling her guts to Matthew over the phone. "Can't. I'm a little shaken by what just happened, I hate to admit." She started the car and turned on the headlights to shine into the trees where Darren had disappeared, then locked the doors. "You won't believe it."

"Believe what?" He lost his jovial tone.

"I went back to the lighthouse to ask Darren a few questions. Chloe has evidence that clears her and Justin."

"What is it?"

She longed to forget their kinky sex tape. "I'll explain in the morning. Anyway, I just don't buy that Darren didn't hear Lacey the night she died. He's a soldier, trained to protect what belongs to him."

Matthew scoffed. "The walls of the lighthouse are solid as steel and if he was in a deep sleep, it's doubtful that he would've heard a thing."

Riley searched the tree line for a man with a rifle. "She must have screamed, right? That would have alerted him."

"That's conjecture. What if Lacey was taken by surprise? One solid hit on the head would make her unconscious. Wham! Then whoever did it could toss her over the platform to the sea below."

"Like a piece of garbage," Riley said sadly. "The woman was no saint, but who did she piss off enough to deserve this?"

She needed to write out a list of suspects, cross off Chloe and Justin, and move Darren to the top.

"Matthew, have you ever been in the presence of someone that chills you through and through? Darren is dangerous." She scanned the deepening night as she turned her car to face the road and moved away from the lighthouse and the threat. Her family needed her, and she them. She was eager to go home now and make sure her family was safe.

"He has plenty of demons and copes the best he can."

"He met me on the property tonight, holding a rifle." She would never forget how comfortable he'd been, stroking the weapon.

"*What?*"

Riley bit her bottom lip as she reached the main road. Safety. "Lighthouse is closed but Darren admitted using Melatonin and that it helped him sleep—sometimes. He says he didn't hear a thing that night."

"Melatonin is a hormone that you can buy as an over-the-counter supplement to help you sleep," Matthew said. "I checked with the pharmacist at the drugstore. It wouldn't change his behavior. I just can't tag him as the killer."

Driving home, she used her rearview to make sure she wasn't followed. "I know you don't want to believe this, but he has the strength to be capable of committing the crime. He was here when it happened, so that immediately puts him on the suspect list. And the man is not right in his head."

"Riley!" Matthew admonished.

"What? Chloe told me that Lacey had been friendly with Darren, back in the day. Did you know that?"

"Lacey was not discriminating in her relationships, if they could even be called that."

She could tell Matthew wasn't taking her seriously and shared, "He may have threatened my family." Five minutes and she'd be home to make sure they were safe.

"Why are you only mentioning this now? What did he say *exactly*?"

She took a deep breath and released it. Staying professional even when her heart pounded with fear. "He...he said he'd seen my mom and daughter, then added 'cute kid.'"

Matthew expelled an exasperated breath. "Darren is just awkward with people. Says inappropriate thing at times. I'm sure he wasn't trying to frighten you. Did he actually point the rifle at you?"

"No." She'd gotten the feeling that he'd been guarding the perimeter of his property. "But how could he have seen them? I thought he avoided people and spent most of his time alone."

"He does, but he's not a complete hermit. Geezus."

She checked the side mirrors. All clear. "How long have you known him?"

"For years. Before he went off to war."

"Matt, you knew Lacey as a teenager, Darren too, and Katie from the bar. Isn't it strange that all of you are here when she gets tossed off that railing?"

His voice hardened. "What are you insinuating?"

Riley realized that she was once again walking a fine line. "Nothing. I just find it curious, that's all." Her brain spun the names around like a kite on a windy day.

"I gotta go," Matthew said coolly. "Katie says hi."

"I'm sorry!" She didn't trust Darren, even though he had a huge fan club on the island. "I just pulled in my driveway. I'll be home for the rest of the night."

"Sandpiper Bay is one of the safest places in the country to live. This is not the norm, all right? We will find who killed Lacey."

"Thanks, Matthew." She turned off the engine and could clearly see her mom and daughter's silhouettes through the living room window. The sheer curtains were closed. She'd order new ones tomorrow.

It wasn't the first time she'd had to act independently of others to do what was right. She wouldn't sleep well until an arrest was made, even if she had to catch the killer herself. And if that killer threatened her family?

She wouldn't guarantee what condition he'd be in by the time they reached the jailhouse.

Chapter Fifteen

"Mom, Kyra?" Riley called as she burst inside the cabin. She left the worry and fears over Darren *mostly* in the Fiat. She locked the bolt on the door behind her.

"We're in the living room, Riley. Hang on, and we will join you in the kitchen."

Her mother's sweet voice warmed her heart, but she knew to downplay her emotions. "Hey, guys! I'm sorry I had to put in such a long day. I missed not having dinner with you." She hugged and kissed her daughter, and with a smile, took her mother's hand.

"I have a nice bottle of Chianti waiting for you." Her mom nodded toward the table. "Next to the two glasses."

"I sure could use it tonight. We can enjoy it next to the fireplace, while Kyra finds us a good movie to watch." She sniffed the air. "Smells yummy. Did you save a little for me?"

"Of course we did." Her mom laughed. "It's in the oven on low."

"We can't wait to hear all about the dead girl," Kyra said, her eyes shining. "Did you find who did it, Mom?"

"I can't talk about an open case; you know that, hon."

Kyra's shoulders dropped and she pouted. All Riley could think about was how Darren had said she had a cute kid. Even moody, Kyra was a cutie. How to keep them out of harm?

Find the killer.

She turned from them to the counter.

"That's all right," Susan said in her role of peacekeeper. "I'm sure your mom is ready for a hot meal and a break, right? Like we talked about?"

"Yeah. Want a comedy, Mom?"

"Sounds perfect." She'd learned to compartmentalize her job and home life a long time ago and relied on that skill now.

Six plastic containers containing the leftovers were already sealed and ready for the freezer. Her mouth watered just looking at them.

"That Maria has quite the personality!" Her mom spoke in an extra-cheerful tone. "She brought over enough food to last a week."

"Best Italian ever," Kyra piped in, standing at Riley's elbow. "Even better than Nico's by our old house, Mom. Everything looked so yummy that I filled my plate with pizza and a big portion of lasagna. I barely touched the salad."

"Maria is a woman you can't say no to. She gives from the heart." Riley pointed to the stairs, eager to get out of her uniform. "I'll shower later, just let me wash up and change my clothes."

"I'll get your plate ready, dear." Susan turned off the oven and pulled her oven-safe mitts on.

"Thank you. I'll have what Kyra had, a taste of everything!" Riley unlaced her boots as she climbed the stairs to her room and bathroom she shared with her mom.

Riley scrubbed her hands and splashed water in her face. She dared her image to reveal any of the fear she'd felt at the lighthouse and thought she'd hid it well.

If her mother had noticed, she'd said nothing.

When she returned to the kitchen she grabbed the bottle of Chianti. The sound of the cork popping was the best thing she'd heard all day. Kyra was in the living room flipping channels. Riley poured them both a glass and slid one next to her mom who was staring at the oven and tapping her toe.

"Why are you just standing there?" Riley handed her the glass and touched the rim with hers. "Cheers. Now we can sit at the table and I'll tell you what I can, but it's not much."

"I will in a sec." She flipped her gray hair behind her ear. "Warming one of Maria's garlic rolls for you."

Riley took her wine and the full plate of amazing-looking lasagna, sided by a generous scoop of ziti, to the kitchenette table and sat. She picked at her food, waiting for her mom.

She spied sausage and onion in the ziti and the scent of oregano and rosemary in the savory sauce. She couldn't resist one tiny bite. And then another.

Finally, her mom opened the oven door and put the rolls on a plate to cool, then sat opposite Riley.

"So, what do you think?" Her mom laughed at the ziti half gone.

The heavenly scent of the buttery garlic rolls got her mouth watering all over again. "If those taste as good as they smell, I don't see myself ever cooking again."

"Thank heavens," her daughter called out, busy searching the videos for their nighttime entertainment.

Riley laughed. "It's time for your Nana to teach you to bake, young lady. And cook dinner on occasion. Fourteen is a fine age."

"I'll be too busy at school, then I'll need to do extra work at home so I can keep my grades up. Four years and then I'm off to college."

"Don't worry, Kyra, I can help you," Susan said with confidence. "Expect it won't take more than an hour since you're so smart." She gave her favorite and only granddaughter a thumbs-up. "I skipped a grade in school so brilliance runs in the family." She laughed and snagged a piece of garlic roll.

Riley had gone from college to the police academy, and it had taken the regular amount of time. Hard work. Study. She sipped her wine. "Guess I missed that gene."

"Think again!" Her mom got up to help Kyra make a decision before it was time to go to bed. The girl could be very picky.

Riley finished her dinner, then got up to rinse her plate before putting it in the dishwasher. She refilled their wineglasses and joined them in the living room. Her mom sat next to Riley and they were cuddled up in front of the fire.

The sight brought tears to her eyes. Being at home with the two of them was like a warm blanket wrapped around her, offering comfort. She had the two most precious people in her life with her on this remote island. She would find Lacey's killer and keep it a paradise.

***

The following morning Riley woke up late and had to skip breakfast in order to get to the station on time. Her mother pushed an apple into her hand and an energy bar. "You need to eat, Riley. Skipping meals is not healthy."

"I ate enough for two days last night, Mom." She swung the door open, feeling about twelve years old. "If you have time, I'd like you to order curtains for the windows. If not, I'll do it this weekend. No biggie."

Her mom started to ask, but then didn't. "I'll do it. We'll be home today to finish our birdhouse project."

Perfect. She'd suggested it last night, thinking she'd been smooth. Her mom *was* brilliant. "Thank you, Mom." She lifted the apple. "Not sure what time I'll be back, but I'll stay in touch."

As she drove, she mulled over everything she knew. This was her normal MO and she'd solved a great deal of cases by listening to what her head was telling her.

Katie, Darren, even Matthew, "Matty", had all known each other when Lacey had lived here with her grandparents. Her mind hummed as if this was an important piece of the puzzle.

What had they gotten into? While the others were still friends, Lacey was not. Darren had motive and the means to have killed Lacey. He was a trained soldier with PTSD, which led to all kinds of other issues.

Katie. What was Katie's story? She'd moved away from the island, but then chose to come back here of all places.

She liked Matthew, but why was he so adamant that Darren was innocent? Did he know more than he let on? As an officer, he was not above committing a crime, as she well knew.

Today was the first day of September, and the weather was a little cooler. Rays of sunshine peeked through the treetops, almost blinding her at times. The locals loved this island. Maria considered herself a local and had been here twenty years. Her suspect list was growing instead of shrinking. Had Maria lived here when Lacey was running wild that summer? Who else knew Lacey and was not happy that she'd come back? She'd broken her grandparents' hearts and the residents here protected their own.

What about Coby? He didn't belong in the inner circle, yet she'd seen his dislike for Lacey herself.

Had Lacey known that her best friend Chloe was sleeping with Justin? There was probably a way to forge a time stamp. Maybe she shouldn't take them off her list.

She needed to talk with Katie and see what information she could share. An early lunch? Katie might not be busy around eleven and could speak freely. Who had been with Lacey that night? Who had Joan seen following the girls Friday night?

Justin. Had he shown up to win Lacey back or to get his revenge? Lacey had broken it off with him so she could start a new life in Vegas. Her best friend Chloe had her own agenda.

Riley pulled up to the station, parked, and rushed inside.

Nancy's head shot up at Riley's frenetic entrance. "Good morning! Don't worry that you're a few minutes late, the boss hasn't come in yet."

"That's a relief. Is Matt still here?" She hoped he hadn't already gone home from the night shift.

"In his office." Her eyes twinkled. "I can see your mind churning from here. Did you find out who killed Lacey?"

"Working on it, Nancy. I need a whiteboard and some markers. Hey, could you make me a list of people you know who lived here when Lacey did?"

"Might take me a little time, but sure. You'll find office supplies in the jailhouse where we store the extras. Want to me to get it for you?"

"That would be a big help, thanks!"

She knocked on Matthew's door and he waved for her to come in. "Hey, Riley. Are you feeling better after last night?"

"I am, thank you." She was too keyed up to sit. "Have you ever had one of those moments when lightning strikes?"

"Is it storming?" He scanned his cell phone for the weather report. "You moved from one high death-by-lightning state to another."

She rolled her eyes at him. "Not literal, thank you. Metaphorically speaking."

"Explain, please." He tipped his chair back and watched her pace.

"Well, we've established the fact that you, Katie, and Darren knew Lacey way back when. She wasn't a decent person. Who else might she have hurt in her past?" Riley placed both hands on his desk and leaned forward. "Matthew, I'm starting to think we need to expand our suspect list."

He straightened and the legs of his chair thunked. "Away from Darren? I'm glad you're starting to see the light."

She hadn't quite said that, but she didn't clarify. It was up to her to make sure that they arrested the guilty party.

"Our job is to wrap this up quickly so everyone on the island will feel safe and can get on with their lives."

"Roger that." Matthew rubbed his hands together. "Who else is on the list?"

"I want to question Katie today. Figured I'd have an early lunch and see how much she remembers from not only the night Lacey was killed, but from when they were kids together."

"Good idea. Want company?"

She didn't jump on his offer. Would Katie speak more freely without Matthew there? "Don't you need to sleep?" she said with a laugh.

"There's a killer on the loose, Riley, in my home. I'll nap and see how I feel in a few hours." He got up and logged out of his computer.

"See you later, then." Riley went to the kitchen for coffee. When she returned, Matthew's office was closed up.

Nancy gestured to Riley's office. "I put the whiteboard in there for you, Riley. Found a few pens but they might be dry."

"Thank you!"

"I'm working on the list between calls."

She would need to bring Nancy back something special for all the extra help. She spent the morning hanging up the board on the wall and making a large list of possible suspects, with Lacey's name in the center.

She'd told her boss that he didn't need to go to Portland to talk to Justin DiCaprio aka Smith, owner of the Kitty Cat Club, because of the time stamped sex photos of Justin with Chloe. Now she wondered if that had been the right call.

It was ten thirty when he returned. Riley went to the chief's office and knocked on his closed door.

"Come in!"

"Morning, Chief."

Riley stood before his desk as he leaned back in his office chair, his hands on his protruding stomach. "How's the investigation? I've had Nancy field calls from the reporters, but word leaks out on this kind of thing."

"I've got a whiteboard in my office that you're welcome to look at. Old school, compared to computer programs, but it helps me think."

"Nothing wrong with the old-fashioned ways so long as they work." He straightened. "Sniders told me that you received a possible threat from Darren

Williams. Tell me what happened. I will not tolerate one of our officers being threatened with a damn rifle."

Her cheeks heated. She relayed what had happened. "He didn't point the gun at me, nor did he directly say that he'd hurt my family."

He tapped the desk in obvious annoyance. "*Cute kid* could be just that. Making small talk."

"He's not very good at it."

"Agreed." Barnes scratched his chin in contemplation. "Why don't you leave the rest of his questioning, if there is any, to Sniders?"

Riley bowed her head, not exactly saying one way or the other. "I'm going to the Lobster Pot to question Katie Hudson. She knew Lacey when she lived with her grandparents."

"Really? I thought Katie came from Canada."

"Her boyfriend's family is in Brunswick, a fishing town similar to ours." How easily that had flowed out of her mouth. *Ours.* Was she beginning to feel at home?

"Huh."

"Katie and Carter were also one of the last people to see Lacey alive. She'd been in the restaurant with a friend of hers, Chloe. Chloe says that Lacey was jealous of Katie."

"The redheaded best friend that was sleeping with the strip club owner in Portland."

"That's the one."

The chief swung around in his leather chair. "There are times I look at my infant granddaughters on video chat and wonder what kind of world we are leaving for them."

She'd never seen him open up like that. "Our job is to make it a better place, Chief. I remind myself of that when I get overwhelmed by it all."

He nodded and held her gaze. "How close are you to getting this solved? I kind of thought a hot shot from the city would have someone locked up by now."

"I'm on it!"

He waved her out of his office with a grunt.

She raced by Nancy, who was still on the phone, and grabbed her keys and wallet to be at the Lobster Pot before Katie had a full dining room.

Food and information were high on her priority list. Once the questions began, Katy might be able to supply a solid list of people who wanted Lacey dead and by the process of elimination, she'd have the killer.

She was singing along with the Eagles during the ten-minute drive. At eleven fifteen, only a few cars were in the gravel parking lot.

Katie was setting tables as Riley entered and looked up with surprise. "Hello, Officer Harper. It's nice to see you again. You here for lunch?"

"Yes. I skipped breakfast."

"Sure," Katie said, as easygoing as Riley remembered. "Want a booth or a seat at the bar?"

Riley glanced around the mostly empty dining room. "Where would it be easier to talk with you? I have a few questions regarding the night Lacey was here."

"Oh." She wiped her hands on her apron, her smile fading. "There will be more privacy at a corner table next to the bar."

Riley took the seat that had been freshly cleaned with a new table setting. "Matthew might join us, so please leave another setting just in case." Riley had been glad to beat him here for this moment alone with Katie.

"Of course." The young woman brushed her dark curly hair back over a plump shoulder. "I don't see a lot of him anymore. He either doesn't like my food or is working too hard."

"He's working night shift this week. I've had your cooking, so I know it's not that," Riley laughed.

"I guess the chief is probably tired of working nights." She looked around. "I'll grab you an iced water while you read the menu, then we can chat until things get busy. I'm the only server on, since Carter is cooking, until noon, then Sarah comes in."

"I appreciate that." Riley picked up the menu, scanning the lunch specials. Should she have lobster bisque and half a sandwich or go for the gusto and get the lobster roll?

Riley considered her choices. She felt the teensiest bit guilty eating here when she knew how much her mom and daughter had enjoyed it and decided to surprise them. Delivering lobster rolls when she finished would allow her to drop in casually to make sure they were safe, and ensure her mom had ordered curtains.

When Katie returned with her iced water and lemon, Riley had made up her mind. "I'd like the clam chowder soup with a small chef salad. And three lobster rolls to take home."

Katie laughed. "Can't forget Susan and Kyra. Sounds like it'll make a good dinner for later."

"Lunch for them, and an office snack for me. My mother made chicken pot pie from scratch for dinner and if we don't eat it, she might quit cooking, and my daughter won't be happy. I'm not so great in the kitchen."

Katie's brows rose and she giggled as gave the order to Carter. "The rolls will be to go," she told him, "and add a big Caesar salad on the house."

"Ah, you don't have to do that!"

"I want my customers to be happy." Katie sat down at one of the three vacant seats. "So, how can I help you?"

"I have learned recently that Matthew, Darren, and you were friends with Lacey when she lived here with her grandparents."

"That's true, although friends might be a bit of a stretch."

"Really?" Riley sipped her water. "Do you mind telling me a bit more about that?"

"Yeah, sure." Katie lowered her gaze to the salt and pepper centered at the table.

Riley sensed that the cheery-natured restaurant owner was very reluctant to share the past, but she was doing it anyway.

"The four of us hung out one summer, but after a few times, no one wanted to do so anymore. She was always taunting us and calling us sissies if we didn't carry out her crazy-ass plans." Katie wiped her palms with a napkin and drew a quick breath. "I wasn't the only one who wanted to get away from her—we all did—but she had a way to make us stay."

That was terribly vague. "What did she do, exactly?"

Katie bit her lower lip and glanced back at the kitchen, toward Carter. "She'd threaten to tell our parents the bad things we'd done, at her instigating. We knew she would. What did she care? Her grandparents were clueless and would never punish her, since her parents were dead." She pressed her hand to her heart. "God, that sounds awful."

Riley patted her wrist with compassion. "What did she have over the three of you that could be so bad?"

"I...it's not *just* my story to tell, you know?"

Riley's imagination went wild with different theories. Just then, the door swung open and Matthew, in casual clothes instead of his uniform, walked through the door.

"Matty!" Katie waved at him in relief.

Matthew smiled shyly at Katie and nodded to Riley. "Mind if I jump in on this?"

"Not at all," Riley answered. She could see Katie's reluctance to give intimate details and hoped that Matthew would help sway her. "Perfect timing."

"What did I miss?" Matthew asked.

"Not much at all. I just got here myself. I ordered the clam chowder and asked Katie here to save you a seat in case you woke up in time." That would show that she was a team player.

Katie leaned toward Matthew. "I was just telling Officer Harper how we didn't want to hang out with Lacey the summer I was here with my family. She pretty much blackmailed us into being her fake friends."

Blackmail was a more serious charge than tattling. "Matthew? What would she have blackmailed you three about?" Katie had already told her, but maybe there was more?

Matthew heard her sharp tone and shrugged, also reluctant to give details. "Lacey was the instigator of the group, as you know. She ordered us to do things no good kids would do."

Riley was ready to scream at the way they were dragging their feet. Unless this was a sex ring or drug trafficking—but she really didn't think that would happen on the island. "Like what? Give me an example."

"Small stuff at first," Matthew confessed. "I was only eleven at the time and my parents had taught me right from wrong. Her first 'test' to be in her club was to steal something out of the market."

"I remember that," Katie said with a blush. "I grabbed a package of gum. I never even chewed it; I was so afraid to have it that I threw it away in our neighbor's can."

Riley smiled softly at Katie, then Matthew. "You?"

"I put a large package of Doritos under my windbreaker."

"Matthew Sniders! I am shocked at you!" she teased. "Figured you as a model child, not a delinquent!" She gave a shake of her head. "You realize that you aren't going to do time for petty crimes as a youth."

"Guess 'she made me do it' isn't a proper defense anymore." Matthew glanced down at the floor, then back at Riley. "Don't know why we let her boss us around like that. Not proud of it, that's for sure."

Riley couldn't help one more tease, since they were both so obviously miserable. "Times have changed. I wonder if it's too late to arrest you two?"

Katie licked her bottom lip, her blue eyes wide. "That's not funny. Trust me, I've never done anything bad except for that one crazy year. And Matty became a cop."

Matthew chuckled. "Wow. All right. Never thought of that before, but maybe that's why."

"I was just kidding," Riley said. "I'm sorry that you guys went through that, but it sounds like normal teen stuff." Nothing to incriminate anybody on her suspect list or explain Lacey's control.

Katie stood up. "Your lunch is probably ready. Matty, do you want anything?"

"Crab cakes and fries."

"Okay, I'll be back in a minute." She hurried off.

After she left, Riley put a hand on Matthew's sleeve. "I know you weren't a bad kid, but what I don't understand is why any of you would want to be in her awful club in the first place."

Matthew's neck grew red. "As you can guess, my ginger hair set me up for teasing and I wasn't the most popular kid in school. I stuttered a lot back then, especially when I was called on to speak in front of the class."

Katie returned with Riley's chowder and salad, then took a seat again. "I heard what you said, but you were wrong. Everyone liked you, Matt. You were just this really sweet guy."

He looked at Katie like she'd grown horns. Ah...Riley sensed an unrequited crush from the school days.

"Matthew, did you think that hanging out with Lacey would make you popular?"

"Kinda. The kids started looking up to me, and the teasing stopped. Classmates and the track team all thought I was a real badass."

His face was so crimson it had to hurt. "And were you a badass?" Riley glanced at Katie to see if she was smiling or laughing, but her expression was somber.

"More than I'd care to remember. Smoking. Skipping school. Forging our mothers' signatures." He grinned and elbowed Katie. "Mine gave me a whooping so hard that I couldn't sit for a week when she found out." His neck flushed a deep red, disappearing below his T-shirt collar.

"That really sucks...or sucked." Katie twisted the paper napkin she held and told Riley, "It's not like we wanted to do the crappy things she asked, but she'd mock us and call us all *candy-ass babies* and threaten to kick us out of the club." Her nostrils flared. "I wish she had tossed us out, you know?"

Matthew winced. "She said it just like that, candy-ass babies. Dang, but that just doesn't have the same bite as an adult."

Carter, who she recognized by glimpses of his dark hair from the kitchen area, brought out the crab cakes and fries and placed them in front of Matthew. "How's it going, man? We haven't seen you around much this last week."

"Night shift." Matthew centered the plate of steaming food. "This looks great."

"Our revenue goes down when you work nights." Laughing, Carter introduced himself to Riley. While he and Katie each had dark hair, his eyes were green while hers were blue. "I'm Carter Jones, Katie's better half. And you're the new policewoman in town. Officer Riley Harper?"

"That's me. It's nice to meet you, Carter. My family and I are huge fans of your cheffing skills." Then she added with a smile, "Katie knew the dead woman, so we're just hoping she'll confess and we can all go home."

When Carter raised his brow and threw Katie a worried look, Matt spoke up. "She's kidding. Got a weird sense of humor. Us at the station think she may have fried it in the desert."

Riley tossed a lemon peel at Matthew and smiled at Carter. "We're just trying to shed some light on who might have killed this woman nobody liked. Can either of you think of someone? This isn't dislike we're talking about but rage, pure and simple."

"Lacey was with a red-haired woman that night," Carter said. "They were fighting about who was going to pay the bill. She ended up doing it, but she was pissed off about it."

"Chloe. That was Lacey's best friend. Did you see anybody else with them? This man?" She took her phone from her pocket and searched her photos for the picture of Justin.

Katie shook her head as she scanned the image, as did Matthew, but Carter frowned and enlarged the photo. "Yeah. I didn't think he was with them though. I thought he was by himself. I only remember him because I thought his mustache was kinda cool. Like a seventies porn star."

Katie spluttered and rubbed her thumb over Carter's smooth upper lip. "I like it this way, babe." She looked over his shoulder toward the front door. "Shoot—gotta go take care of the lunch crowd, but Sarah will be here in a few minutes if you have more questions for me, Officer..."

"Call me Riley, please. We understand you have a business to run, so thanks for your time."

Katie and Carter split in different directions—Katie to the hostess stand for menus and Carter to the kitchen.

Matthew picked up his fork and dug into a crab cake.

"I think it's wonderful that you turned your bad experience as a kid into being a cop," Riley said. She meant every word. "Is there more? I'm only asking because right now, it doesn't seem like enough to make three kids go against their upbringing."

"Yeah." Matthew dragged his hand over his forehead and down his cheek, then settled it on the table next to his plate. "You're pretty persistent in your questioning, Riley."

"I'm not here to judge, and I won't, but I just need to know what Lacey was capable of—give me the worst, Matthew."

He sat back. "It was a progression; you have to understand. It went from stealing to be part of her club, to skipping school, smoking, drinking, and all trying to hide it from our parents who had no clue. That was the worst, lying to them."

"Where did you meet?"

"The lighthouse."

"I knew it!" Riley smacked the table. She finished her chowder, feeling like she was on the right track. Lacey had died at the same spot she'd forced them all to meet.

Matthew bit a fry in two. "We got pretty good at sneaking out that summer, among other things."

"So." Riley shifted on the chair. "You say that Lacey controlled you all because you wanted to be in her club. You were friends outside of the group?"

"More like allies trying to survive a battle. Darren was a few years older, like Lacey. Thinking back, I'm sure they were hookin' up in the woods. Katie and me were younger and didn't know. Deke and Margot were in between us and Darren in grades."

"What woods? Mackabee's?" She watched Matthew as he squirmed beneath her stare. There was a story there. She actually felt sorry for him and the stuttering kid he'd once been that a bully like Lacey had taken advantage of. She'd guess that Katie had been targeted as well as the others. People like Lacey were heartless manipulators who behaved without conscience to get what they wanted. "What happened?"

"This was like the third time she wanted us to all meet in the woods, at the fisherman's lodge. To party. She said we were going to have a new ritual to bond us all together." Sweat dotted along his brow despite the AC in the restaurant set to arctic. "We were going on a hunting expedition. I figured she meant a deer or something and didn't want any part of it, even though my dad used to bring home a buck every year." He wiped his mouth. "When we got to the lodge. God." He swallowed. "It wasn't deer she was after."

Riley was getting a crystal-clear picture of who Lacey had been. A certifiable psychopath. "Then what did she want?" Her stomach tensed.

"We were all to split up. Lacey gave us each a pocketknife, with all this ceremonial chatting crap, and told us to go kill something and bring it back. Whoever had the biggest creature would win a prize."

He drank his water until he'd emptied the glass, parched and shamed from his confession.

"Did you do it?" Lacey was an awful, awful person.

Matthew lowered his head and his voice. "I brought back a toad that I'd snatched off a tree. Stabbed it. I had nightmares for years."

It was no wonder. "The others?" Riley glanced at the cheery Katie who smiled in their direction as she spoke quickly with another woman in an apron. Sarah.

"Margot brought back a caterpillar that she'd obviously just found. Lacey laughed and tossed it in her face, excommunicating her from the club. Deke had a squirrel that he'd nearly beheaded. Katie had a worm that didn't wiggle anymore. Darren brought back a dead snake, wrapped around his hand like a boxing glove. He won."

Of course he had, Riley thought. "Who else was in your group?"

Katie arrived, putting her hand on Matthew's shoulder. "There were seven at first, but then just six." She thumped her temple as if that might bring the name up to the front of her brain. "Steve? Stephan?"

"Stanton," Matthew said sadly. "Lacey teased him about being a dweeb."

"That's right. Stanton Fleming. He wore glasses and had a cowlick. He wanted Lacey's approval even more than the rest of us did."

Riley jotted his name down in the notes app on her phone. Stanton Fleming. Margot. Deke. "Deke works for Captain Wyatt, right? Do you remember Margot's last name?"

Matthew and Katie both shook their heads.

"You realize that Lacey manipulated you by preying on what she considered a weakness. They weren't. Look at you both. Successful. You have wonderful lives filled with purpose. Chloe said Lacey was jealous of you." It wasn't the woods that were evil, but people.

"Looking back now," Katie shrugged. "We should have stood up to her."

"You were kids," Riley reiterated. Could their guilt have caused them to kill Lacey when she'd come back to the island? She prayed not. "Lacey thrived on having you in her power."

Katie nodded and patted Matthew's shoulder. "Back then we were all a little afraid of her. She seemed bigger than life. And cruel. What if she hurt our families in retaliation?"

Matthew sighed. "In a perfect world we could have told our parents and gotten Lacey in trouble. Saved ourselves from her. But we're living on an island with no easy escape. We all know each other and help our neighbors. My parents were good friends with her grandparents."

"Tell me what happened after the night in the woods."

Matthew and Katie exchanged a look. "I stayed home until it was time to go back to Canada," Katie said.

"I had the longest case of the flu known to man," Matthew said. "The next year was high school and Lacey had moved on. I was still in middle school. What a relief."

"Did you all talk about it?"

"No," Matthew said. "None of us spoke about it back then."

Riley had a hard time believing that. "Why is that?"

"People around here protect their own," Katie said. "They don't snitch."

Chapter Sixteen

Matthew stroked his chin as Katie said the words, *they don't snitch*. Riley remained rooted to her seat.

Would she ever be able to outrun what had happened? To her knowledge, Katie didn't know of her past scandal, unless Matthew had told her.

Had the two of them been more than friends? Would they cover for one another? While the woods story was heinous, was it true or were they playing Riley to hide their own dark deeds? She didn't believe that for a moment. No.

Riley released a calming breath, not letting the phrase shake her as it had done at Piazza Piper with Maria.

"Sometimes letting it out is the right thing to do. From what you've said, Lacey had a serious mental disease."

"We were kids," Katie said with a self-deprecating chuckle. "What did we know? It actually feels good to get this crapola out in the air after so long hiding it. My mom found out some of the stuff I'd gotten up to that summer with Lacey, and I wasn't allowed to come back the following season. They sent me to a camp in Colorado instead."

"I'd wondered why you never returned!" Matthew said.

"Horseback riding and wilderness training." Katie patted her curvy hip. "Best diet ever, fish and berries. I know how to build a great campfire. It was fun."

Riley smiled. "So why did you start a business in Sandpiper Bay?"

"Fond memories of my good times here. With my family and grandparents. I don't mind saying that I asked around and heard that Lacey was in Bangor and then Portland. The price is right for a startup."

"The weather doesn't bother you?" If she had the freedom to go anywhere in the world, Riley was pretty sure that an island that got snowed in wouldn't be her top pick.

"No. It's less fierce than Carter's hometown of New Brunswick. Talk about brutal cold!" She shivered and chattered her teeth.

Riley looked out the window at the blue sky and darker blue ocean. "Right now, it looks too beautiful to be brutal."

"Weather here can change in a snap," Matthew said. "We have another two weeks or so. I'm already noticing a nip in the morning that hints fall is on the way."

"I noticed too!" Riley said.

Carter came out with Riley's to-go bag. "Thank you very much!" She turned to Matthew. "I'm going to drop this off at the house, and then I'll be back to the station. What's your plan for the afternoon?"

"Headed home for shut-eye before my ten p.m. to six a.m. shift."

"I prefer our hours," Carter said. "Right, Katie? Here at nine every morning to start the baking for the day."

"And it feels like we never leave," Katie only partially teased.

"I like the night shift, usually." Matthew shrugged. "Things are peaceful."

"Except the other night, with Lacey," Riley said, keeping the subject on the dead woman. She'd only known Matthew a week. "What made you turn yourself around?"

"Freshman year of high school. I joined ROTC. I made new friends that I actually liked. Who liked me. Turned out I was super accurate on the target range. I found a girlfriend who didn't mind my hair." He rustled the short locks.

They all laughed.

"What happened with Lacey?" Riley pulled her wallet from her pocket.

"I quit seeing her around," Matthew said. "I wasn't surprised when she ran off at sixteen. She didn't fit on the island, but this is my home, you know?"

Riley checked with her gut and didn't think Matthew had anything to do with Lacey's death, but as he had said himself, he probably knew the killer.

He was emphatic that it couldn't be Darren, but she wanted proof of the ex-soldier's innocence before she cleared him. After all, he'd killed a snake to win the prize for Lacey.

She had a feeling that there was a clue hiding in the group of misfits from so long ago.

She stood up and handed cash to Katie to cover the bill for her food and a tip. "Keep the change. Thank you."

"See you later," Katie said. Carter smiled benevolently at her.

Matthew raised his hand but stayed to finish his crab cakes.

Riley brought the bag of lobster rolls to the car and started it up, ruminating over what she might be missing.

The teenagers had been coerced into bad choices in order to be popular. Matthew had turned himself around. Katie had been sent to Colorado, away from Lacey's clutches, and now owned a restaurant with a loving boyfriend.

Darren had joined the military. Deke stayed local and worked at the ferry station. Stanton. What had happened to Stanton Fleming? And she'd need to ask Nancy if she knew a Margot.

She drove to her cabin, parked, and ran inside to put the food in the fridge for later.

"Anybody home?"

The television was off, and the house felt empty. Her mom had said they'd stay home to finish the birdhouse. Apprehension filled her. Were they okay? She put the lobster rolls in the fridge and peered out the window.

She was hit with a pang of love and relief when she saw her daughter and her mother in matching kayaks on the edge of the water, having fun.

"My turn later, after I find who killed Lacey," she told herself, hustling back out to the car. The sooner she did, the sooner she could relax and not worry about her family innocently enjoying the outdoors. Soon it would start to snow and they'd be locked in the house due to inclement weather.

Riley recalled her words to the chief—it was their job to make the world safe for those they loved.

She was back in her office by one that afternoon, searching her whiteboard for the truth. Lacey's name was in the middle. She put psychopath underneath it in red.

Nancy had left some names on her desk, but she was out to lunch. Riley scanned it but the list was two pages long. She fired up her computer. The chief's office was dark, and she could hear Rosita in the kitchen. The woman loved her fizzy water.

She typed in Stanton Fleming, Sandpiper Bay.

She expected the usual social media pages. What she got was an obituary notice.

"Dead!"

"Who is?" Rosita asked from Riley's open doorway.

"Did you know Stanton Fleming?"

Rosita was in her late forties and not in the same crowd as the others. Coby was the same age, but he hadn't grown up here.

"No. Is he a local?" Rosita entered her office and admired the whiteboard.

Riley scanned the obit. "He was born here and moved away with his parents at thirteen to Bangor."

Rosita stood over Riley's shoulder. "Is this important to the case?" When Riley didn't answer, Rosita asked, "How did he die?"

"Says here it was a car accident." Riley read farther and her heart ached. "Him and a train."

"Oh. How sad. When?"

"God, he was only twenty-three." Riley finished reading the article. He had a history of reckless behavior. "He was in and out of drug rehab." Could that be laid at Lacey's feet?

Rosita cracked a can of something mango. "Why were you interested in him?"

Riley scooted back from the desk to look up at Rosita. "He was part of the crowd hanging out with Lacey the summer that Katie was here. She had them doing some rotten stuff. The rest of them turned their lives around." She thought of Darren and his PTSD. "More or less."

"You mentioned Katie and Lacey. Matthew. Who else?"

"Deke. Darren. Stanton. Margot."

"Deke's another one who's done good," Rosita said. "I know his mother really well and she spent plenty of sleepless nights worrying over him. He got the job with Captain Wyatt on the ferry and shaped up."

Riley raised a brow before Rosita had him relegated to sainthood. "I hear he still hits the bottle pretty hard."

"Lots of folks around here do that and manage all right." Rosita grinned. "My poison of choice is tequila."

"I'm not much for hard alcohol. I like wine, though, and the occasional beer."

"We all have our vices," Nancy said, having heard the last part of the conversation as she walked toward Riley's office with a pink message pad, obviously returning from lunch. "I like donuts. All kinds, but especially the Bavarian cream." She peeled off the top sheet and bypassed Rosita. "S'cuse me. Here you are, Riley. Darren called for you."

Chills raised the hair on her arms. "What for?"

"He'd like you to go out to the lighthouse. He wants to show you something."

"Did he say what?" That sounded ominous.

"No." Nancy smiled. "I know he's an odd duck, but war changed him. There is still a sweet man under all the scar tissue."

"He was one of the kids that hung out with Lacey that summer fourteen years ago. Did he stay on the island or leave, like Stanton?"

Rosita raised a brow. "Darren joined the military right after high school. He's two years older than Matthew. I only know that because I was part of the welcome home committee when he came back."

"He looks a lot older than thirty."

"War will do that to you." Rosita's mouth thinned. "No way did he have anything to do with Lacey's death."

Riley shook her head in frustration. "He has a lot of support from folks around here."

"He's one of us." Nancy squeezed Riley's wrist. "Give him a chance. Go talk to him."

"Want me to ride with you?" Rosita asked, probably sensing that Riley was hesitant. She didn't mention the possible threat. *Cute kid.* It could have been nothing.

The words themselves were innocent enough.

"No. Thanks. I'll go. Nancy, thanks for the list." She picked it up and scanned it, but the names didn't mean anything. They were all familiar, or not. "Did you happen to know a Margot who would have been about the same age?"

Nancy sucked in a breath and blinked watery eyes. "Margot Ludwick. She drowned her freshman year in high school. It was terrible. I was friends with her older sister."

There were a lot of dead people turning up around the island. There had to be a connection. "I just want to watch the videos one more time. I'll return them to Captain Wyatt after seeing Darren."

The women nodded and left Riley's doorway. She followed Rosita down the hall, and then Rosita went into her office.

Riley walked to the old-fashioned VCR and powered on the TV and the machine.

Nancy sat at her desk. "You looking for anything in particular?"

"Not exactly," she said with a rueful chuckle. "Makes it difficult."

"Right? Well, if you think of anything I can do to help, just let me know."

"You've done so much already—thank you."

Riley watched the ferry crossing again. There was Deke in a navy-blue cap tossing bread to a gull to make a little girl laugh, grinning at the camera. He'd gotten a smile from Kyra with his juggling skills—not an easy feat. Captain Wyatt clapped his hand on his head to save his white hat from flying off in a gust to the sea. How many trips did the man make a day? What did he see? A lot, no doubt. There was the burly man who mishandled the luggage. Coby showed up in quite a few of the videos. Where did he go? He'd made it sound that first day as if he rarely left the island.

Lacey had arrived in Sandpiper Bay a week ago tomorrow. She slowed the film. There was Justin, hiding in the background, watching Chloe and Lacey from the shadows. Creepy.

But not guilty.

She watched both tapes on warp speed and finished in an hour. She'd learned nothing new. She pressed the eject button on the VCR and put both cassettes in a brown paper Sandpiper Bay Police Department bag.

"I'm off to Darren's," she told Nancy.

Nancy looked up from whatever she was doing on her computer. "Keep an open mind."

"I know. I hear you. He's one of yours."

"Yours too, now," Nancy said with an admonishing smile. "You keep saying for the next year, but maybe if you didn't think of it like that, the time won't pass so painfully."

Riley straightened. Had she been giving out that temporary vibe? If so, she was as guilty of not trying as Kyra.

"You're very observant, Nancy."

"I'm a mom."

"A good one, sounds like. I'll take some pointers and adjust my attitude."

Nancy blushed. "Oh! It wasn't a criticism."

"An apt observation. No offense taken." Riley grabbed her purse from her office and slid her fingers around the handle of the bag of tapes. She decided to leave a note for Matthew in his office to call her when he came in, even though it would be late. Had he known that Margot was dead? He had to have known, and yet he hadn't mentioned it at lunch.

His office door was closed but unlocked, so she went in and searched his desk for a piece of scratch paper. She accidentally moved the blotter and her heart stilled when she saw Lacey's name.

Was this how he worked, jotting down notes? Riley felt caught between snooping and detecting and wished she hadn't come in, that she hadn't seen this. She sat in his chair and opened the folded paper.

Oh, Matthew. You're pretty smart.

He'd also put together Lacey and the old gang, even Margot. He'd drawn a stick figure named Lacey in the center, with spokes like a wheel coming from it, with names of those from his childhood. Margot and Stanton each had a line through their name. Matthew had a line through his. Lacey was crossed out, which left Deke, Darren, and Katie.

So where was he now? She put the paper back beneath the blotter. Did he know who was guilty, and was he taking matters into his own hands? He had feelings for Katie even if they were not returned in that way.

"You all right?" Rosita asked as she entered the hall from her office. "I thought you were going to visit Darren."

"I am. Right now." Riley left Matthew's office and strode past hers to the lobby and the front door.

"Good luck," Nancy said shyly.

Riley waved goodbye and got into her car. She needed more than luck. She'd take a miracle.

She placed a call to Matthew. This was a nightmare come true, having to question the motives of a fellow officer. The call went to voicemail. Damn it.

Within moments she'd arrived at the lighthouse where she parked and got out. It wasn't dark yet, but the sun was fading behind a cloud. She knocked on the yellow door. "Darren?"

No answer.

Odd.

She searched the property, calling for Darren. What had he wanted from her? Why on earth would he call her out here, only to disappear?

Riley stood on the sharp edge of the hill leading down to the beach. She heard a swoosh, and then two hands pushed between her shoulder blades, knocking her off the cliff.

Chapter Seventeen

Riley rolled down the rocky hillside, her breath knocked out of her. Stars danced before her eyes as she tried to suck in air.

No dice.

Her head swam as she lay on her back and stared at the gray sky. Why had Darren pushed her? Why had he called her? To confess?

She sipped air through her nose, slowly, then parted her mouth to gulp it in faster. Her lungs ached and cramped before she settled into normal breaths. Good, deep yoga breaths.

Her hands were cut on the rocks. Something warm dripped down her cheek. She realized that she'd landed by the same rock where someone had folded Lacey's clothes.

She focused on a prone figure on the beach, the face splashed by water as the waves came in and out.

Light-brown hair, darkened by water. A bristled jaw. Darren?

She scrambled to her feet in confusion. Had he jumped after he'd pushed her? Riley shielded her gaze and looked up toward the lighthouse.

A man scurried down the path toward her with a bellow of fury. Silver glinted at his brow. It wasn't Matthew. Who the hell else could it be?

She dragged Darren's body backward out of the surf so that he didn't drown and searched the beach for a place to defend them both.

In Darren's hand was a navy-blue cap. Caps. She remembered the day when Lacey had arrived, when the tourist had his cap stolen by the seagull. Riley had been on that boat with her family, not Lacey. Her mind fitted the last piece together. That cap belonged to the second mate on the ferry.

Deke. She'd been right about the death having something to do with Lacey's bullying that awful summer.

She hadn't taken her own advice to look for actual proof before mentally condemning someone, like Darren, when she should have been open-minded to see that Deke had actually physically matched the criteria.

The "abrasions" on his arm when he'd juggled for Kyra had matched the rash on Chloe's arm from the poison ivy. He must've gotten it when he'd folded Lacey's clothes, to set up Darren for the crime.

Deke had killed a squirrel. A living, breathing animal. That was psychopathic behavior, as was acting like nothing was wrong. No signs of guilt because he didn't feel guilty but empowered.

He'd smiled into the camera, knowing it was there. He and Lacey were two of a kind.

Riley unclasped the holster on her gun but didn't draw her weapon. She mentally played her possible responses as she watched him take the last few steps down the path. He had something in his hand—it looked like a rock. Lacey's head had been bashed in.

She would act like she was on defense, but in reality, Deke was going down. Taser, baton, pepper spray, gun, cuffs. Her wits.

She pretended like she couldn't put weight on her ankle as she stepped back.

He grinned, his gaze flat. "What took you so long to get here, Officer? I called over an hour ago. Tide's comin' in. Darren's gonna drown. I've got it all arranged to make it look like he attacked you when you came to arrest him, but he can't die before you. Somebody might actually catch on."

So, he'd been the one to call and set up the meeting through Nancy. Not Darren. "I was watching some video from the ferry. You were there. You're always there, aren't you? The ferry allows you full freedom to come and go. Nobody questions your actions."

His smile fled and his expression flattened to match his cold eyes. "Captain Wyatt told me you'd taken the tapes. Which ones?"

What had she seen specifically to alarm Deke? "Interesting viewing."

Darren's outstretched fingers twitched. Was he coming around? Could he help her? Or did he need an ambulance?

"Where are the tapes?"

The last thing she'd tell him is that they were in her car. "I just dropped them off at the ferry depot."

"Yeah? What did Wyatt say?"

"He was with a customer," she bluffed. "Worried, are you? That you're connected to Lacey?"

His jaw clenched. "Knew her as kids. We all did. Too bad Darren here went crazy and had to kill her out of revenge," Deke droned.

She stepped in front of Darren. "Too bad. Too bad nobody's going to believe that. Darren here is a wounded soldier who's made his mark in this town. He's got allies. The chief. Matthew. Me."

Deke hefted the baseball-sized rock in his palm.

She kept her hands to her sides... She could reach her weapon and draw in seconds.

Deke moved toward her.

He was surprised when she stepped his way.

A smile danced around his mouth.

"Interesting move, Officer Harper. I kinda expected you to be a weakling, being as you ratted out your fellow cop. It was all the islanders could talk about before you got here."

She swallowed her reaction, not wanting to show weakness. "I did what was right for me and my family. I would do it again. The law is the law. I swore an oath to uphold it."

He tossed the rock a few inches in the air and caught it.

Don't show fear. What had she seen on the video? Lacey hadn't talked with Deke on the ferry. What had seemed innocent enough perhaps hadn't been. Had he taken her snub as a deliberate slight? Had that sparked his rage?

What about Margot, his teenaged girlfriend? Deke was charming in his own way, easygoing. He'd gotten a smile from a reluctant Kyra.

Ted Bundy had charmed the ladies. Her stomach churned. She'd bet Deke was worried because there might evidence of his flirtations, or worse, on those tapes.

"Lacey thought she was too good for you, didn't she?" Riley said. "A stripper at the Kitty Cat Club."

Deke winced. "Lacey had potential, but in the end, she was just a slut. No better than the others." He tossed the rock and caught it.

How many "others" were there?

Riley laughed in a mocking way. "I saw the tape when she came over with Chloe. She was flirting with everybody but you. She had a real man. A man who owned a business in Portland. Why on earth would she waste her time with you?"

Deke's eyes glittered with the hint of madness. "She's dead. Lacey had to die."

"No, Deke. She didn't."

"She was going to tell."

"About...the woods?" That was kid stuff, not worth killing over, unless there was more.

"Margot," Darren croaked from behind her.

Deke grimaced and raised the rock. "Shut up!"

"You killed Margot?" Riley repeated. His first kill, but not his last. He'd made it appear like a drowning. He was cunning. She had to make sure that he would kill no more. She took a step and winced, faking an injury to her ankle as she hobbled on one foot.

Deke lunged for her with a triumphant grimace. Riley was knocked backward as she tripped over Darren's body.

Just what she wanted, to be close to Deke. She had her taser free and jammed it into Deke's side, activating it as they rolled over and over on the sand.

He yowled and her fingers stung. Deke kicked it from her hand and wrapped his fingers around her throat in a choke hold.

She let her body go limp, then when he relaxed, she pulled her gun from her holster and brought the muzzle beneath his chin. She thumbed back the hammer.

"Don't move," she ordered.

He froze. "Bitch."

She didn't blink. It was up to her to keep these creeps behind bars.

Darren stumbled upward but then raised his hands. "What do you want me to do, Officer?"

"Call Chief Barnes. I'm going to bring in Deke Anderson once I arrest him for the murder of Lacey Killian. And Margot. And we need to confiscate all the tapes at the depot to search for evidence linking him to any other questionable drownings of young women."

"Sluts." Deke glared at her but wisely didn't say any more.

***

Riley had to wait for the chief to bring the patrol car and while she cooled her heels, she cuffed Deke and grilled Darren, since Deke wasn't talking.

She ushered him before her up the path to the lighthouse parking lot. Darren was right behind her. She kept her gun trained on Deke as she had him lean against her tiny Fiat.

"Tell me what happened here, Darren."

Darren gave a single nod but was quiet as he gathered his thoughts.

"When did you find out that he'd killed Margot?"

"I suspected when I heard the news, but I was at boot camp when it happened. Margot doted on Deke, but Deke had a thing for Lacey. Lacey, being Lacey, tormented Deke. Teased him. She was a bitch."

"Not acceptable to kill her even if she was cruel," Riley said.

Darren nodded. "I know. We've all been talking at Katie's place. About what to do."

This explained why Matthew had been so protective of Darren. And Katie. "But you weren't sure that Deke was guilty?"

Deke growled at him to shut the hell up. "Lacey was a bitch," Deke said. "And a slut. She was going to tell the cops about Margot!"

"And she didn't want anything to do with you," Riley surmised. "That had to hurt, huh, Deke?"

Darren shuffled his feet on the sand, one shaky hand in his hair. "We had to be sure. We take care of our own."

"We couldn't get enough of each other then," Deke said with a laugh. "Kinky shit. There was no other girl like her. Not even Margot."

Riley didn't lighten the pressure of her hand on her gun. Deke was the monster she was most concerned with at the moment. "Were you following Lacey Friday night? You were seen by a witness. Did she invite you to be with her and Chloe, or were you spying?"

Deke jerked his chin at Darren. "I was making plans to set this jackass up."

Darren's anguished gaze skipped from her to Deke. "What did I ever do to you? I tried to help you get into the service."

"You left this rock. Returned a hero." Deke strained against his cuffs. "You're no hero."

"I agree with you," Darren muttered. "I was just doing my job."

"That makes you a hero in my eyes," Riley said. "A soldier protecting his country." She thought back to Chloe saying how Lacey was jealous. Maybe Deke had been too. "What's the matter, Deke? You didn't pass the physical to get into the military?"

His eyes blazed with fury.

She nodded, more to herself than Darren or Deke. "Matthew became an honorable man and a police officer. Darren, a soldier. Katie, a business owner.

You killed poor Margot. Then there's you and Lacey. Losers. I think Stanton was more like you two as well."

"So?" Deke asked.

"That had to really burn you up. Not as good as Darren or Matthew. And then Lacey returns, a stripper, and she won't give you the time a day. Ouch."

"She's a viper," Deke said. "I'm glad she's dead."

Riley raised her brow at Deke. "Is that a confession?"

His nostrils flared. He whirled around and tossed his weight at her, knocking her off-balance.

Darren's eyes grew huge in his pale face.

Deke tried to run, but Riley had chased down scumbags all over Phoenix and was used to dirty tricks as criminals fought to get away.

She swept out her leg, tripping Deke to land in the sandy dirt. She jumped on his back and yanked his cuffed hands higher, just as the chief pulled up in his SUV. Matthew was behind him in the patrol car.

Barnes got out as Riley lifted a cursing Deke. "We'll add resisting arrest to your sheet," she said.

"Well done, Officer Harper."

"Thanks, Chief. Deke was snubbed by Lacey, who he deemed a slut. He's worried about the tapes, so we should confiscate them all to see what he might have on there that he doesn't want us to know about. I think he's been killing around the island since a girl named Margot. Psychopaths are known to keep a trophy of some sort."

"Where are they?" Chief Barnes rocked back on his bootheels.

"Two are in my car. I was gonna drop them off with the captain after seeing Darren. Darren, I'm sorry I doubted you."

Deke tried to get free, but Riley had a firm hold. "Give it a rest," she mumbled. "Before you hurt yourself."

Matthew grinned and opened the back of the patrol car. "Your ride, Deke."

Riley hustled Deke into the car.

"Meet you at the station, Officer Harper," Matthew said.

She glanced over her shoulder to where Barnes was talking with Darren. "Matthew, I saw your notes about Lacey in your office. You're a smart cop. What were you going to do about Deke?"

Matthew shuffled his feet. "I wanted concrete proof before we turned in one of our own. Guess what I found at your place just an hour ago, Deke? Lacey's cell phone."

Deke blew a raspberry. Riley slammed the rear passenger door. Jealousy was never pretty.

Matthew drove to the jailhouse behind the department. She walked to her Fiat where the chief and Darren were talking.

"What a first week in Sandpiper Bay. I thought it would be nice and quiet."

The chief snorted. "It usually is. And then you showed up."

Riley wasn't sure if that was a joke or another personal attack. With a new positive attitude, she chose to believe the first.

The End.

AUTHOR BIO: PATRICE WILTON

NEW YORK TIMES, bestselling author, PATRICE WILTON knew from the age of twelve that she wanted to write books that would take the reader to faraway places. She was born in Vancouver, Canada, and had a great need to see the world that she had read about.

Patrice became a flight attendant for seventeen years and traveled the world. At the age of forty she sat down to write her first book—in longhand! Her interests include tennis, pickleball, traveling, and writing stories for women of all ages.

She is best known as a popular romance author with 35 heartwarming stories on her resume. She is especially proud of her bestselling contemporary romance series, Paradise Cove, Heavenly Christmas, and the Wounded Warriors. Co-writing with Traci Hall, they have assumed the name Traci Wilton for the Salem B&B mystery series published by Kensington.

AUTHOR BIO: TRACI HALL

From contemporary seaside romances to cozy mysteries, USA Today bestselling author Traci Hall writes stories that captivate her readers. As a hybrid author with over fifty published works, Ms. Hall has a favorite story for everyone.

Mystery lovers, be on the lookout for her Salem B&B Mystery series, co-written as Traci Wilton, and her Scottish Shire series, which takes place in the seaside town of Nairn, as Traci Hall.

Whether it's her ever popular By the Sea series, the next Appletree Cove sweet romance, or a fun who-done-it, Traci finds her inspiration in sunny South Florida, by living right near the ocean.

Writing as Traci Hall, Scottish Shire mysteries

Murder in a Scottish Shire July 2020

Murder in a Scottish Garden May 2021

Murder at a Scottish Social 2022

Traci Hall also writes historical romance, western romance, teen paranormal, new adult paranormal, coming of age, and non-fiction books.

Go to: TraciHall.com to learn more

OTHER BOOKS BY TRACI HALL AND PATRICE WILTON—Written as TRACI WILTON

Mrs. Morris and the Ghost August 2019

Mrs. Morris and the Witch 2020

Mrs. Morris and the Ghost of Christmas Past September 2020

Mrs. Morris and the Sorceress March 30 2021

Mrs. Morris and the Vampire August 2021

Mrs. Morris and the Pot of Gold 2022

A Note from the Authors

Thank you for reading DEATH IN SANDPIPER BAY
If you enjoyed this book, I'd appreciate it if you'd help others
find it so they can enjoy it too.
- Lend it: This e-book is lending-enabled, so feel free to
share it with your friends.
- Recommend it: Please help other readers find this book
by recommending it to friends, readers' groups, and discussion
boards.
- Review it: Let other potential readers know what you liked
or didn't like about.
If you'd like to sign up for TRACI WILTON'S newsletter to receive
new release information, please visit www.traciwilton.com
THANK YOU

www.ingramcontent.com/pod-product-compliance
Lightning Source LLC
Chambersburg PA
CBHW021000180726
47993CB00017B/472